High Society Gangster III

The Final Chapter

Thomas Long

Nothing lasts forever. Every epic series must come to an end. I hope all of my readers that have enjoyed the previous installments of the High Society Gangster series will enjoy the grand finale. I appreciate your support!

------T. Long

Chapter 1

From the moment he was placed in the back of the squad car, Geno sat quietly with a pensive look on his face. He paid no attention to the two federal marshals responsible for transporting him as they talked amongst themselves. They were engaged in conversation he found to be meaningless. His mind was focused on trying to figure out how he wound up in this position. He was totally out of his element. He kept seeing images of Carina and his children with a dazed looked on their faces as they stood in the driveway of their home while the federal marshals carted him away to jail. Their images played over and over in his head like the remote control to the DVR was stuck on rewind. The expressions on their faces filled his heart with intense feelings of sorrow and regret. This was a day he wished he could take back and start all over again, but he couldn't.

It had been over twenty years since he last had any interaction with law enforcement on this level. He was just out of his teens at the time and he swore from then on he would never return to that dreadful place. Up until this point, he made good on his promise. As an attorney, he was the one used to getting his clients out of police custody with his brilliant legal maneuvering. Now, he would need the help of one of the qualified attorneys at his law firm to represent him in this case. Even though he was a beast in the courtroom, Geno knew it would be foolish to try and represent himself. That would be suicidal for any attorney, let alone one with a resume like his.

Geno had just the right person in mind to handle this case for him. Solomon Price, a young lawyer he took under his wing right after he graduated at the top of his class four years ago from the University of Maryland's Law school, was who he planned to appoint as his legal counsel. His father was Jewish and his mother was African American. Solomon grew up in the mean streets of west Baltimore with his mother and two older sisters. His mother couldn't afford to pay to send him to college so he paid his way through school with scholarships and by working full-time in a warehouse for a local furniture company.

Geno was introduced to Solomon by Paul Giannetti, a lawyer colleague of his whom Solomon had interned for while in school. Solomon impressed Geno with his work ethic and the charismatic way he could make legal arguments to sway a jury. He reminded him of himself early in his legal career. He wasn't too cocky or brash, but he was self-confident enough to know he could hold his own doing battle with any other opposing attorney at law. He was also a quick learner and good at preparing thorough legal case briefs. These were just some of the qualities Geno loved about him. He planned to give him a call once he was given an opportunity to do so.

"So, you're the great Geno Caprese, huh? You're supposed to be such a powerful wise guy, but you don't look like a tough guy to me. In fact, you look more like a square kinda fella," Federal Marshal Remington Jibbs stated mockingly.

A pale skinned Caucasian male in his early fifties, he had been on the force for over fifteen years. Prior to becoming a federal marshal, he was in the Marines for a decade before he was honorably discharged. He was in the driver's seat and briefly took his eyes off the road to glance in the rear view mirror in Geno's direction. He wanted to see if he could get a rise out of him.

"Yes, I'm Geno Caprese. However, I never claimed to be a gangster or any other form of criminal. Those are your words not mine. That's a title that you alphabet boys came up with to try to stereotype all of us good, hard working Italian American citizens. I'm an attorney and a businessman and nothing more. Everything I have I got from hard work. However, judging by the way you gentleman invaded my home and frightened my children, I could argue that you guys are the real goons or gangsters. You treated me like I was some kind of terrorist or something. You're obviously acting off of misinformation. You men should be ashamed of yourselves accosting a hard working American citizen like myself. If you don't mind, I prefer to keep the conversation to a minimum until we get to where we have to go," Geno replied rather smugly. His attempt to play the good guy sounded quite convincing. He almost had himself fooled. Jibbs' words got under his skin, but he handled it well. Under different circumstances, he would love to get Jibbs in a boxing ring so he could test his mettle as a man because he was totally out of line to call him a square.

"If you're a legitimate businessman, then I'm a fucking pirate. You can tell that story to the Judge. I know you're just another street punk dressed up in a fancy suit. You and your people cause mass destruction in our communities with your drugs and feel no guilt about the lives you ruin. We've had you on our radar for quite some time. Now that we've finally nailed your ass, I can't wait to see how you handle life behind bars. Jail is a totally different world from the way you're used to living in that big mansion with the super sized bedrooms, expensive European cars, the Olympic sized swimming pool, and all of that other fancy stuff. In jail, all you get is three hots and a cot. You won't be sleeping on Egyptian cotton sheets either. You might run your little crime family, but when you go to jail the Warden has the final say on all things. Pretty boys like you don't do well in the joint. I could definitely see you becoming some big Black guy's little bitch," he shot back at Geno, further antagonizing him.

"If I'm the person you think I am, then it would be wise for you to just do your job and let me be. I think that would be in your best interest. Sometimes when a person talks too much they have a way of talking themselves into situations where their words end up costing them more than they expected," Geno quickly replied.

His response to Jibbs was more a statement of fact as opposed to just an idle threat. He had the ability to have Jibbs eliminated without even batting an eye. Geno was not in the mood for small talk or to entertain his foolishness. For Jibbs to question his street credibility was unfathomable to him. Clearly, he did not understand the amount of mayhem he could rain down on him with a simple phone call.

"Look at this, the big bad gangster, Geno Caprese, has me shaking in my boots over here! I don't need you to tell me what's in my best interest. Again, you're in my custody right now. I set the rules here. I say what goes and what doesn't. It would be wise for you to remember that fact Caprese," Jibbs said in a threatening tone.

"Have it your way, big fella. You win. I'm just a nobody. You're the man. I surrender. I just want to get this over with as quickly as possible," Geno rebutted.

It was senseless for him to argue with Jibbs. He had bigger fish to fry like making bail and planning out his legal strategy for this case. He knew that the federal agents had already ransacked his home looking for evidence and assumed that the Caprese Foundation's office was next on their agenda. Geno wasn't worried at all because their search would turn up nothing. He never kept any records of his illegal dealings in either location. He was too smart to do something so foolish. However, he was curious to see just what evidence the Feds had against him. It was his best guess whatever they did have was something they manufactured themselves to get a conviction against him. He saw it happen enough times before with his clients and he would find out soon enough if he were a victim of the same type of underhanded tactics.

"Jibbs, relax man. Why don't you just let Mr. Caprese be? He is not causing us any kind of a problem at all. We're just doing our jobs, Mr.

Caprese. This is not personal. I apologize for my partner's rudeness," the other marshal, Trey Wingate, interjected in a seemingly sympathetic tone. His partner took the hint when he realized Trey wouldn't co-sign his attempt to get Geno riled up. Jibbs eased up on antagonizing Geno any further.

Trey, still in his early thirties, grew up in the Baltimore area. He was very knowledgeable about the notorious reputation of the Caprese crime family. He didn't want any problems whatsoever with a gangster like Geno. His partner was a hardnosed agent who lived and died for the job, but Trey just saw the job as a nice paycheck and federal pension that he planned to live off of in his retirement years in the distant future. He wasn't interested in making enemies. To get into a beef with a dangerous man like Geno was not high on his list of things to do. Jibbs could continue on with the lip wrestling and slick talk with Geno if he chose to do so. Trey just wanted to make it through his shift safely so he could go home and enjoy life outside of work.

"I appreciate you saying that, young man. Maybe your partner could learn a thing or two from you," Geno suggested.

Jibbs didn't say a word, but shot Geno the look of death. He hated men like Geno who played both sides of the law. He hoped he would rot for the rest of his years in a jail cell. In his eyes, Geno was nothing more than a low life hood who was about to get what he deserved. He planned to be in attendance for his entire trial to witness him get his just due.

The entire ordeal thus far seemed unreal to Geno and he could foresee it only getting more bazaar. One minute he had visions of relaxing in the sunshine on a tropical beach with Carina and the children, and the next minute he was being whisked away by an army of law enforcement officials. His paradise had turned into a nightmare without any kind of advanced notice.

Geno was beyond furious. He felt embarrassed his children had to see him being arrested. That was the last image he ever wanted for them to have to witness. He created a reality for them whereby committing a crime and going to jail were two things they would never have any reason to find themselves involved with at any time in their lives. His children looked at him as their hero and to see him being arrested made him feel as though his image was now tainted in their eyes. The last thing he wanted to do was to disappoint Gianna and Stefan. In his absence, he knew Carina would do her part as the matriarch of the family and explain the situation as best she could to the children.

In his world, Geno Caprese was the voice of authority and the undisputed king of his domain. He got his clients acquitted of criminal charges and it was beneath him to be the one who faced federal indictment and a possible long prison sentence. To take away his freedom was akin to taking away his ability to breathe. Jail was not a place for a man of his level of intelligence and business expertise. Even though he came from the streets, he was far removed from interacting with the law on the level of facing jail time like the crew of street level workers who followed his every command.

Geno was sure he had thoroughly insulated himself from ever facing prosecution for his criminal misdeeds, but the handcuffs around his wrists currently indicated he had clearly miscalculated his position in the world. No amount of money could totally wipe away the possibly of him going to jail if somebody in law enforcement had it in for him bad enough. This was a hard lesson for him to learn. Reality had its own way of making a believer out of the most pessimistic souls. This dose of reality served as a wakeup call for Geno.

When the federal agents invaded his privacy and stormed onto his property to arrest Geno, they had no idea what they had done. They created an enemy out of a man who refused to bow down or submit to any form of authority. Being placed in handcuffs awakened a beast inside of Geno he had tried his best to put to rest with his efforts to further penetrate corporate America and become an accepted and influential member of the upper echelon of the financially elite class of this society. The sheer notion he faced incarceration enlivened his gangster persona that he worked so diligently to replace with the image of Geno the attorney and businessman. That other person inside of him was hell bent on exacting revenge and punishment on the person or persons responsible for his current predicament. He came up with countless ways he planned to make those poor souls pay for making his life uncomfortable at the moment.

It seemed like an eternity before they made it to the Bureau's headquarters. When they reached their destination, Jibbs pulled the car into a parking spot and they got out to escort Geno inside. Geno's eyes lit up when he saw the swarm of news reporters on the front steps already positioned to bombard him with questions. Apparently, somebody had already tipped off the press about his arrest in an attempt to embarrass him and tarnish his reputation, but Geno didn't care. He was eager to seize the moment and make a statement to the press to profess his innocence, but his escorts didn't give him a chance to do so. They whisked him by the crowd of reporters as fast as possible and into the building so he could be processed into custody expeditiously.

Once Geno was led inside of the building, the madness continued. He passed by other marshals and federal employees who stopped and stared at him as though he was a superstar like Michael Jackson. A part of Geno was flattered by the attention, but he didn't let it distract him from his current reality. This was a serious situation and required all of his attention. Once he was placed in an interrogation room, he sat alone for about 30 minutes before the door in front of him opened and a familiar face stood before him. His entire disposition changed. He shook his head in disbelief and disgust. The man in front of him was none other than his arch nemesis in the courtroom, federal prosecutor Gavin Mayhem.

Geno rocked back in his chair, stretched out his arms wide, and let out a large sigh of relief. To know Mayhem was involved with his arrest indicated he was in for a rollercoaster ride. This case was clearly motivated by Mayhem's personal disdain for him. Nonetheless, Geno was ready to take on the challenge once again. He had whipped Mayhem in court so many times, he was sure this instance would be no different. He was sure he was ready for whatever drama he tried to bring his way. He looked him directly in his eyes with the same piercing look on his face as he had done so often before and Mayhem didn't flinch one bit.

"Mayhem, what is this all about? Did you miss me? You still haven't gotten over how I spanked you in the Jackson brothers case recently, have you?" Geno jabbed at him with a smile on his face.

He lived to taunt and mentally torture Mayhem. It gave him a cheap thrill to know he could easily ruffle his feathers. However, today, Mayhem didn't seem to be phased by his antics. He had a wide grin on his face and appeared to be in an unusually relaxed mood.

"The Jackson case is old news, my friend. You can rest assured I've put that one behind me. This smile on my face is for another reason. I finally have you right where I want you to be. You're one slippery son of a bitch, but this time I've got you dead to right. It brings me great joy to know you will be spending a long stretch inside of a jail cell like you deserve to do. It's not the charge I wanted to nail you with, but I'll take what I can get," Mayhem bragged.

He reached down inside of his briefcase and pulled out two large manila folders. He placed them down on the table in front of Geno for him to view. Geno picked up the folders and glanced over the materials. His face got tighter after every page he turned. He couldn't believe what he was reading or that Mayhem was able to get his hands on such potentially damaging information. Only one other person knew anything about the financial transactions detailed in Mayhem's documents. Geno was stunned that Sam Bradford could betray him after all he had done for him. He had made him a ton of money over the years that allowed him to live a rather plush lifestyle and to be stabbed in the back was the thanks he got in return. He felt disappointed and furious. Nonetheless, he couldn't let Mayhem know he had him in a noose right now.

"What the hell is all of this nonsense? Mayhem, you have nothing on me. I don't know anything about any of this money mentioned in these documents here. This paperwork has nothing to do with me. Why are you wasting my time?" Geno shot back at him defiantly.

"You see, Geno, before I didn't have any hard evidence on you to get a conviction, but this time I flipped somebody in your organization. He's willing to testify against you in exchange for immunity. That person gave me the rundown on all of that dirty money you've been hiding. The account numbers and paperwork show me a trail to all of the fake shell companies you set up to hide your dirty money. We have it all. You're going to have to explain how you failed to pay taxes on all of that money for so many years. Geno, your reign is about to come to an end, my friend. You're done," Mayhem uttered confidently.

He chuckled in Geno's face because he clearly had the upper hand. He watched Geno once again look over the evidence he had compiled about his illegal financial transactions and noticed his facial expression change from a dismissive one to a look of genuine concern. All of the evidence Mayhem had was circumstantial because Geno's name or the name of the Caprese Foundation was not on any of the legal documents that he read. However, the fact the Feds had Sam Bradford as its star witness made the evidence hard to refute. Sam happened to be responsible for handling a significant amount of the Foundation's financial dealings. He could provide a detailed account of every back door deal he did on Geno's behalf. Mayhem finally had the smoking gun he needed to convict him.

Never could Geno have ever imagined he would have to endure another backstabber in his midst. First Silvio, his own brother, hatched a scheme with his enemies to kill him and now, Sam Bradford, a trusted board member, decided to become a federal informant. While there were some individuals he did business with who had a legitimate axe to grind with him due to some of his unscrupulous business tactics, he always played the game fair with his business associates within the Foundation. Geno always made sure his whole team was well fed financially. He insulated his entire team from prosecution by surrounding them with the best legal team money could buy, but that still wasn't enough to keep him safe from harm. Geno began to seriously question who he could really trust within the Foundation and in his life in general. The amount of time he now faced because of a snitch was enough to make any man become paranoid.

For the first time ever, Geno appeared to be rattled. This was a sight Mayhem had waited many years to see. If he could get a conviction against the great Geno Caprese, it would be the defining chapter in his legal career. Mayhem reveled in the moment. He thought about the legacy he would leave behind if he were successful in bringing down an organization as large as the Caprese family. With the evidence he had in his possession, this was his case to lose. He planned to make sure he covered all of his bases so no mistakes were made. He knew how crafty Geno could be in finding loopholes in the law, but he intended to beat him at his own game this time.

"This is bullshit. Whoever gave you this information is trying to set me up. Nowhere in this paperwork do you see my name or the name of my corporation. I have nothing else to say to you, Mayhem. I want to talk to my attorney," Geno stated defiantly. He slammed the folder shut and sat back in the chair with his arms folded. Things just got real because the information Mayhem had was legitimate. Somebody within his inner circle snitched on him and he knew exactly who it was.

He planned to somehow make an example out of Sam Bradford. His freedom and the future of the Caprese Foundation were on the line. When he was done, Mayhem left Geno behind to ponder about his future. While Geno would spend the night in a stale jail cell, Mayhem was going home to a warm meal and to rest in his comfortable bed.

Chapter 2

"Mrs. Caprese, what do you have to say about your husband's arrest? Is he guilty? Did you have any idea that he was hiding all of that money?" the voice on the other end of the phone asked Carina.

"You lousy bastards leave me and my family alone, Goddammit! Stop calling my home!" she yelled into the receiver before she slammed it down on the kitchen counter.

It had only been a few days since Geno's arrest, but the pressure from the press constantly hounding her had begun to weigh heavily on Carina's mind. Her nerves were jittery. She went to bed every night with a pounding headache. She barely slept at all. Everywhere she went, from taking the kids to school to trying to go to the grocery store, Carina was harassed by the media in an attempt to get her to make a statement of some kind about Geno's legal situation. Her security detail did their best to serve as a buffer between Carina and the media, but news reporters and the paparazzi were relentless. Helicopters flew over the Caprese estate with photographers leaning out of them in an attempt to get photos of Carina and the kids. A few other reporters tried to climb the gate around the property to get an exclusive story from Carina only to be thwarted in their efforts by Geno's armed guards. The media was filled with eager vultures that would do anything for career advancement. They tried to turn Carina's life into a circus and she was at her breaking point. Lucky for her, Jericho had a top notch team of men in place to secure her and the children's safety.

Carina did her best to remain strong throughout the drama, but she missed her Geno badly. Her heart ached for him. Geno was no saint and was probably guilty of the charges being made against him, but she didn't care because this was part of what came along with the being the wife of a gangster. If she was there with Geno to enjoy the extravagant lifestyle he provided for her and the kids, then she would definitely be there for him through rough patches like this one. Carina had no plans to abandon him. She and Geno were one. If he had to do time, she would be right by his side faithfully until his release date. She married Geno for better or worse. He was her King. She would follow him to the ends of the Earth. Carina yearned to see him walk through the front door of their lavish home and wrap his strong arms around her. Tears streamed down her cheeks as she prepared dinner for Gianna and Stefan. She was so distracted she didn't hear Stefan walk up behind her.

"Mommy, don't cry. Everything is going to be alright. Daddy is going to be home soon. If they don't let Daddy go, I'm going to break him out of that jail myself," Stefan stated boldly and sincerely in an effort to comfort his mother. He meant every word. If there was a way he could set his father free, he would do it in a heartbeat. Stefan wrapped his tiny little arms around Carina's waist to embrace her. His head rubbed up against her belly. His gesture warmed her soul. His tiny little arms weren't Geno's, but for the moment they would do.

"I know, baby, everything is going to be alright. Look at you, being a big boy by comforting your Mommy. Your father would be so proud of you. You don't have to worry about breaking your Daddy out of jail because you know your Dad is Superman. He'll be home soon enough. Now go get your sister and tell her it's time to eat," Carina replied.

"Okay, Mommy, I'll be right back. Watch how fast I can run. I'm faster than lightning," Stefan stated, filled with youthful energy. His little feet moved swiftly as he raced out of the kitchen and up the stairs to get his sister. He looked like a miniature replica of his father. Stefan returned a few minutes later with Gianna. Thus far, Gianna hadn't said much about her father's arrest. Her silence troubled Carina because she knew how close they were. Whenever Gianna was quiet, Carina knew something was wrong. They all sat down at the dinner table to have a meal. Carina did her best not to notice Geno's empty seat at the head of the table, but his absence was too obvious.

"So, how was school today?" Carina asked to try and make small talk.

"It was great. I got an A on my math test," Stefan replied excitedly.

"It was horrible for me. Everybody was talking about Daddy. They were calling him a gangster and saying he was a bad man. I almost got into a few fights because I don't play around with anybody talking about my father. Mommy, is Daddy guilty of what they say he did? Is he really a bad person?" Gianna asked. Her eyes were watery and she looked to be visibly shaken up. Carina hated to see her in such a fragile state.

"Baby, you don't have to worry about a thing. You know your father is not a bad person. However, there are people in this world who can't stand to see a man like him be successful. They will do anything to try and tear him down. They can't stand to see us living so well because God didn't bless them to be able to acquire wealth like your father did. None of what we have came easy. He works hard for everything he has given us. Don't let anyone tell you anything different. This whole mess will go away very soon," Carina replied confidently.

"That's right, Mommy, my Daddy is the best Daddy in the whole wide world!" Stefan proclaimed proudly.

"Yes, he is, baby", Carina confirmed.

Truth to be told, Carina had no clue how this would all play out because she had never been in this situation with Geno before. She was just as nervous as Gianna was, but she couldn't let it show. She planned to get down on her knees tonight and pray like she never did before that God would deliver Geno out of this mess and bring him home to be with his family.

"I'm glad to hear all of those rumors aren't true. If one of those girls at school says one more thing about my Daddy, I'ma get suspended for punching her in the face. I'm a Caprese and I don't play around with anybody disrespect our family name," Gianna stated bluntly. Even though she was a pretty and prissy girl, Gianna wasn't afraid to get her hands dirty to defend her father if necessary. She definitely inherited his feisty spirit.

"Calm down, baby girl. You know your father would not want you fighting anybody. He would be upset if you got any marks on that pretty face of yours," Carina joked. Gianna had to laugh as well.

"You're right, Mommy. When is he coming home? I just miss Daddy so much," Gianna whined like the spoiled little Daddy's girl she was.

"He'll be home real soon. We have to let his lawyers do their job, baby, and just be patient," Carina replied.

Carina had to project the strong image of confidence for the sake of her children, but her soul was heavily burdened. Thanks to Geno, they all had grown accustomed to a certain standard of living. He always gave them the best of everything. His current legal situation threatened to take it all away. However, she knew her husband and he wouldn't go down without a fight. He hadn't survived this long without going to jail by being a fool. She knew Geno was a resilient man who always kept a few tricks up his sleeve for times like this. She planned to touch base with Sal in the morning to see exactly where things stood with Geno.

While they sat and enjoyed their meal, the intercom system chirped to let her know somebody was at the front gate. Carina got up to look at the security monitor and smiled when she saw who it was. It was Cesare and Jericho. She walked toward the front door to let them in. They would certainly be a pleasant sight for her weary eyes to see.

Ever since Jericho agreed to work for the Foundation, he and Cesare had become inseparable. After the initial awkwardness of them finding out they were brothers with different mothers wore off, they began to spend more time around each other and developed an instant bond. Cesare took it upon himself to give Jericho a crash course on the things he knew about the inner workings of the Foundation. Jericho was receptive to the information and soaked it up like a sponge. Being around each other so much made them both take note of just how much they had in common. Shavon was away in Connecticut at school so Cesare proved to be a welcome addition to Jericho's life.

Jericho had promised both Shavon and Nina that he was done with the professional hit man business when he went to work for Geno. The lifeline Geno threw him came along at just the right time, especially since Nina gave him the news recently that he was going to be a father. Even though he never had a father figure to show him how he should treat his son, he planned to do everything he could to be actively involved in every aspect of his child's life. He knew he couldn't do that in his former line of work because of the high level of danger and the amount of his time each job required of him. He came to the realization that if he wanted something different in his life, then he would have to take a leap of faith to do something different.

Thus far, his job as the head of security at the Foundation was a breeze for Jericho. It was perfect for him to best utilize the skill set he learned from so many years working under Gutta's tutelage. He was in the process of training all of Geno's current security team with some of the many tricks of the trade he learned from Gutta. Geno placed his personal safety and the safety of his family in his hands and Jericho didn't plan to disappoint him. He made sure he had a cadre of diehard, loyal soldiers under his command to keep his new family safe. With Geno now in jail, this was now more important than ever.

Jericho truly enjoyed the relationship he had begun to develop with Carina and his newly discovered niece and nephew. Carina's female intuition and motherly instinct gave her the vibe that Jericho had a good heart, but it had been tainted for so many years by his understandable bitterness toward Leonardo. She was all about family and believed family took care of one another. As a result, she welcomed her new in-laws with open arms.

Shavon was happy to have a strong female influence in her life to bond with and to share girl time with on occasion. She was also elated to get to know her niece and nephew. Nina wasn't left out of the mix because Carina had to feel her out to see if she was a suitable partner for her brother-in-law. Thus far, Carina liked what she saw in her. She appeared to have the same unwavering loyalty to Jericho as she had for Geno.

As for Gianna and Stefan, they were happy to have a new aunt and uncle. They didn't fully understand how their grandfather kept them a secret for so many years, but their young minds didn't harp on the issue for long. They both thought their Uncle Jericho and Aunt Shavon were two cool individuals. The fact they were African American didn't matter. Geno raised his children to not see race as a barrier to people being family.

"Hey, what are you guys doing here?" Carina asked curiously after she opened the door to let them in. She gave both of them a hug.

"We just stopped by to check on you to see how you were holding up," Cesare replied.

"Are those guys at the front gate doing their job keeping the press out of your hair? Let me know if I need to tighten up security," Jericho offered. If there was a problem, he would rectify it with haste. He took his job seriously. Geno paid him well and he made sure he got his money's worth.

"You don't have to worry, Jericho. We're fine. Look at you, being all overprotective. I'm doing as good as can be expected given the circumstances. Do you guys have any good news for me?" she asked.

"You know Geno has the best lawyers from the firm on the case. He will be home sooner than you think, Sis. He'll come out of this situation with the upper hand like he always does. It's the Caprese way," Cesare stated confidently.

"I have no doubt Geno will be released soon and be back home with us. We were just about to eat dinner. Are you guys hungry?" Carina turned to ask them.

"I'm always hungry for some of that good food you cook," Jericho replied.

Even though it had only been a short time since he met Carina, she had a way of making him feel comfortable around her to let his guard down some. That was a major thing for Jericho because he had trust issues and didn't take to meeting new people too easily. However, Carina's outgoing personality and warm spirit made it hard not to love her. It was certainly out of Jericho's element for him to be spending quality time with his niece and nephew because his social circle had always been just him, Shavon, and Nina. However, once he met Gianna and Stefan and spent some time interacting with them, their youthful energy brought out his inner child which had remained dormant inside of him for so many years. He was becoming a more outgoing person each and every day. Shavon told him all of the time about the positive changes she noticed in him since Geno came into his life.

"Well you two might as well come on in and join us. The kids would love to see you," Carina stated.

They all walked back into the dining room. Gianna and Stefan's faces lit up when they saw their two uncles. They both got up out of their seats to give them each hugs. They all sat down at the table, said a prayer, and talked as they enjoyed the delicious meal Carina prepared. Even though Geno was currently behind bars, with a strong family unit like this behind him, there was no way he could lose. The Caprese family had his back for better or worse. Their bound was rock solid like family should be.

Chapter 3

"Are you okay in there?" Special Agent John Mancini yelled up the stairs from the first floor.

He could hear grunts and groans as the man struggled to relieve himself in the bathroom. Sam Bradford, the man he was responsible for guarding, had been back and forth to the restroom all night long because of an upset stomach. The walls and the floorboards of the old federal stash house were thin. Mancini could hear every step Sam took when he paced back and forth across the floor all night long. His upset stomach was a tell tale sign of his bad nerves. After guarding so many federal witnesses who went through the same thing before testifying in court, he was use to this scenario.

"I'm fine. Can't a man take a crap in peace?" Sam uttered back at him.

"John, leave that man alone. The poor guy can't help himself. As for you, get your ass back over

here and take this whipping I'm about to give you,"
Special Agent Robert Gelasco yelled.

"Don't count me out so fast. I always keep a
trick up my sleeve," Mancini replied.

He walked back into the living room area and
sat back down at the table so they could continue
their game of poker. The two men had worked
together as partners for over a decade for the
criminal investigation division of the IRS. They had
busted numerous high profile individuals for
income tax evasion throughout the years.

A handsome Black male in his early fifties, the
dramatic twists and turns in his life recently added
another ten years to Sam Bradford's physical
appearance. His eyes were bloodshot red. He had
easily visible bags under them. Sleep was the
furthest thing from his weary mind since his arrest.
He was desperately in need of a haircut and a
shave. He had lost at least fifteen pounds in the last
month because he was unable to hold any food
down due to his bad nerves. He spent most of his
days in the bathroom either vomiting or on the
toilet. When he finished handling his business in the
restroom, he washed his hands and walked
downstairs to the area where Mancini and Gelasco
were located.

"You two think you're comedians, don't you?
You think my situation is funny?" he asked clearly
irritated.

Gelasco and Mancini both turned and glanced in his direction and cracked up laughing right in his face. They clearly had no respect for Sam as a man. He was just another scumbag who committed a crime, but sadly didn't have the balls to do the time for his illicit acts. Instead, he chose to set somebody else up to take a fall in exchange for a lighter sentence. To ridicule him was just a part of their daily routine to pass the time. They were responsible for guarding him for twenty-four hours per day. They took turns sleeping so that at least one of them was always alert and on point.

"Hey, it's not our fault that you have the bubble guts. You should've thought about that before you broke the law. You were bold enough to play the game with the big boys, but not bold enough to face the consequences for your actions. You get no sympathy from me," Gelasco replied. He didn't try to hide his lack of respect for Sam.

"You two are assholes to laugh at a man when his life's in danger. I thought you took an oath to serve and protect. Where's your compassion?" Sam tried to reason with them.

"You just flushed our compassion down the toilet," Mancini joked. Gelasco shared in the laughter as well.

"You want us to feel sorry for you because you got caught breaking the law and to save your own ass you turned into a snitch? Get the fuck outta here, Sam. Take your ass back upstairs in that bedroom and watch TV or something. You're starting to pluck my nerves," Gelasco uttered.

Sam mumbled a few curse words under his breath. He walked into the kitchen and looked inside the refrigerator as though he was about to grab something to eat. However, after he received a few shooting pains in his stomach, he decided he just wanted to go lay back down and sulk in his misery. He walked back upstairs to the bedroom with the look of a defeated man. The stairs made an annoying, creaking sound with every step he took.

When he made his way back up to the bedroom, he sat down on the edge of the bed and reached over onto the nightstand to grab the half full bottle of Tums. He popped a handful of tablets into his mouth to try and calm down the bubbling sound of his stomach. Dressed in just a wife beater and pair of sweatpants, he looked more like a homeless bum than the prestigious and well respected man who ran the largest African-American bank on the East Coast. He fidgeted with his watch and constantly checked the time. Every second of each day seemed like an eternity.

Sam's entire being was consumed with fear and with good reason. He put himself in the crossfire of the most dangerous and powerful man in Baltimore City. He wished he could kick himself in the rear end because he had messed up his life royally. His own greed and insatiable appetite for wealth made him make the mistake of a lifetime. Up until this point, he had never been so reckless in all of his years working in the banking industry. All it took was one mistake to set an avalanche of madness into motion. He made that foolish mishap which landed him in the jam he currently found himself in. Being a snitch was a dishonorable brand he placed on himself for a lifetime.

Because of his careless decision making, Sam was now a marked man. Geno told him over and over to thoroughly vet everyone he did business with and he normally heeded his advice. The one time he chose not to exercise extreme caution in deciding who he chose to launder money for proved to be a costly mistake because it landed him in his current predicament. He went from living in a spacious mansion in a gated community in the wealthy Montgomery County section of Maryland to being holed up in crappy little shack not too far away in Prince George County. He wasn't proud of his decision to become an informant, but he had no choice because he wouldn't last a day in jail. He wasn't cut out for life behind bars. He would be an easy target for all sorts of abuse and extortion.

Sam had laundered money for a large number of seedy individuals, from organized crime figures to well respected legitimate businessmen who wanted to hide their earnings, through his bank for years. Up until this point, he had no problems with the law because he was extremely cautious with the manner in which he accepted and processed their money through his bank. He also had connections with bankers and real estate investors in foreign countries as a part of his money laundering network who knew how to make dirty money look clean through the use of fictitious shell companies and other resourceful means. Sam's expertise in this arena was the primary reason why Geno chose for him to be a member of the board for the Foundation. He was a great helper to him in building up the financial portfolio of the Caprese family's extremely profitable empire. However, now he turned into its greatest liability with the amount of damage he could do to its financial infrastructure with the testimony he planned to give in court.

Sam was introduced to Manuel Lopez by a childhood friend named, Peter Bergman. He told Sam that Manuel was a wealthy Mexican philanthropist who needed help setting up legitimate business ventures in the United States. Peter neglected to mention that Manuel happened to be a member of the Lopez Brothers Cartel, one of the most notoriously violent drug cartels in Sinaloa, Mexico. Sam didn't bother to find out on his own either because once Peter mentioned he had over twenty million dollars of Manuel's money to play with, all Sam saw was dollar signs. He envisioned how much money he could make off of the top when he filtered the money through his bank. His affiliation with Geno and the aura of the Caprese family being untouchable by law enforcement made Sam feel complacent and as though he had no worries.

Because he failed to do his due diligence and run a background check on Manuel, Sam had no idea Manuel was a fugitive wanted by the DEA in association with a string of bloody murders resulting from the deadly feud between the Lopez Brothers and their chief rivals, the Nunez Cartel. The feud between the two warring factions spilled over from Mexico into the United States in states like Maryland, Texas, and Miami as splinter factions of their organizations in America battled over drug territory. The bloody murders associated with their beef attracted a lot of attention from the DEA and FBI and brought them into their line of fire as priority targets for prosecution. Violent drug wars were never good for business in the bigger picture because once the Feds had you in their scope, it was hard for anybody to make money without risking arrest.

Peter went to college with Sam and went on to become a successful accountant after he earned his degree. When Sam first opened the bank, he brought him several clients who were into shady business dealings that needed to clean up their dirty money. However, Sam had no idea that over the years Peter had developed a nasty cocaine addiction which led him to dive deeper into the drug culture. It also led to him selling drugs to support his habit and to finance his high octane partying lifestyle. Things got so bad for Peter that he was now no longer an accountant, but a full-time drug dealer. Manuel happened to be his drug supplier. Peter was recently arrested for trying to bring five kilograms of cocaine from Mexico into the United States.

In an attempt to avoid jail time, Peter agreed to give up his connect, Manuel. He also mentioned to the federal agents he knew someone who laundered money for the most notorious gangster in Baltimore City, Geno Caprese. Sam foolishly bragged to Peter in several of their conversations about his affiliation with Geno. When this information was brought to the attention of lead federal prosecutor, Gavin Mayhem, he agreed to give both Peter and Sam full immunity if their information led to Geno's head being placed on a silver platter. It was the slam dunk case Mayhem had worked for years to build against Geno and he would do whatever was necessary to make it happen. He wanted Geno bad enough to sacrifice just about anything. To be able to snag Manuel Lopez as well would be another feather in his cap.

When the federal marshals came to arrest him, Sam cried like a baby. They showed him the video surveillance footage they had of him accepting cash money from Peter. He heard the taped conversations he had with Peter about the ways he could launder Manuel's money and knew he was screwed no matter what he did. If he refused to cooperate with the Feds and give up Geno, he would go to jail for a long time. Going into the federal witness protection program was his only option if he wanted to stay alive and free.

Even though he was now under the watchful eye of the federal government, Sam still didn't feel safe. He feared the wrath of Geno Caprese every day because he knew how well connected Geno was on both sides of the law. He didn't look forward to sitting on the stand and having to look Geno in the face when he testified against him. Honor and loyalty were everything to Geno. He expected nothing less from all of his board members or anybody he chose to associate with in business or his personal life. Geno stated countless times at board meetings, in not so vague terms, that if he ever caught any of the board members in violation of that code of honor, his vengeance would be brutal. Everyone in the room clearly knew what he meant. They all had no reason to doubt his sincerity of purpose if anyone dared to cross that imaginary line with him. Sam had now crossed that line. Geno's words played over and over in his subconscious mind day in and day out.

When Mayhem informed Sam that Geno had been arrested and was in federal custody, he knew it wouldn't take Geno long to figure out he was the informant the government had to testify against him. He expected Geno to be furious and was sure he would come up with some sort of plan to try and get to him. He couldn't wait for this trial to be over so he could start a new life with a new identity in a new location. It wasn't how he planned to spend the rest of his life, but Sam grew to accept he had to make the best out of bad situation.

Until this was all over, he lived with the fear of meeting a violent death at the hands of the Caprese family. That threat was real and something he couldn't let slip out of his every conscious thought even though he had federal protection. To know his fate rested in the hands of two idiots like Mancini and Gelasco did nothing to set his mind at ease. He reclined back on the bed and turned on the television to try and distract himself from the paranoid thoughts that constantly ran through his mind.

Chapter 4

The federal courtroom in downtown Baltimore was packed to capacity. News reporters and camera men were everywhere. They were eager to get either a glimpse of or an epic sound bite from the infamous Geno Caprese. The entire scene was monumental. The crowd of onlookers eagerly awaited his arrival. The level of anticipation and anxiety in and around the building was similar to what one would see at the appearance of a rock star. That was because in the eyes of many in the city of Baltimore, Geno Caprese was a larger than life figure. He was the people's champion.

Geno had a polarizing persona that some people loved and others hated just as intensely. In the hood, Geno was looked at as a legendary icon because he allegedly came from the underworld, but was able to infiltrate corporate America by doing it his way. In other more upscale social circles, there were individuals who saw him as just a street thug who didn't deserve to live in a multi-million dollar mansion or to drive around in the fancy cars he owned. Either way he was viewed by people, Geno knew how to draw a crowd and to captivate the public's attention. He was a magnet for the spotlight. He used it to his advantage every chance he got.

When Geno was escorted into the courtroom by two armed guards with his wrists in handcuffs, he gave the people exactly what they wanted. The man of the hour had arrived. Dressed sharply in one of his custom designed suits, he flashed his winning smile to the crowd and displayed the same cocky swagger and unshakeable confidence about himself that won over juries over and over again throughout his legal career. He wanted to send the message he had no worries and knew he would be acquitted of all charges even though the deck was currently stacked against him.

Geno understood the importance of maintaining a stern poker face in times like this because public perception was everything when one's character was being called into question. He played up to the crowd as the flashes from the cameras went off to capture this historic moment. Geno Caprese, the master litigator, was about to do battle with the federal government in a fight for his freedom. His fate rested in the capable hands of young Solomon Price. This was his chance to show he belonged in the big leagues. The stage was set for an epic legal battle to take place.

As he made his way up to the front of the courtroom, his eyes locked in with Carina's. She was seated in the front row, flanked on both sides by Cesare and Sal. He winked his eye at her and blew a kiss in her direction. He mouthed the words "I love you" and she did the same. He knew this whole ordeal was rough on her and his children. Once he made it out of this situation, he planned to make it up to them in grand fashion. Geno gave a nod of confidence to both Sal and Cesare before he took his place next to Solomon. The scene in the room was intense. Everyone awaited the arrival of the Judge so that the proceedings could begin.

"That's a sharp suit you have on, young man. Appearance is everything in the courtroom. The jury likes to see a well dressed attorney who knows what he is doing. It gives off the vibe of a winner. You see Mayhem over there? That suit he has on came from the thrift store. He looks like a low balling loser," Geno spewed out cockily and loud enough for Mayhem to hear him.

"You can make all the jokes you want, Caprese, but I will have the last laugh this time," Mayhem promised him.

He wasn't impressed with Geno's antics. He was armed with some damaging evidence that he planned to let do the talking for him. Geno's comments drew laughter from many in the courtroom, including Sal and Cesare, but Solomon maintained a serious look on his face. He had a look like he was ready to go to war for Geno. If he were able to get Geno off on these charges, it would go a long way in pleading his case to one day become a partner in the law firm. He had to take advantage of this opportunity and work it to his maximum benefit.

"Geno, we need to be focused. Let's not antagonize the other side. We have our work cut out for us. The first thing on our agenda is making sure we get a decent bail set for you," Solomon advised him.

"You're right, Solomon. I don't know what I was thinking. This is your show. I'ma let you do your thing. This is your chance to show me why I hired you to be a part of my legal team," Geno uttered calmly.

He was initially offended by Solomon's statement, but then he came back to his senses. Solomon was right to advise him to tone down his behavior. He would have told his client to do the same thing given the situation. He also had to remind himself that Solomon wasn't under his tutelage at the moment. He was his attorney in the courtroom. He had to trust that his every action and thought was in his best interest as his legal counsel. After this trial was over and Geno was acquitted of all charges they could sit back, smoke a cigar, and have a good laugh, but for now, this wasn't the right time for jokes. They had a brief conversation about legal strategy before they were interrupted by the Magistrate Judge entering the courtroom from his chambers. Geno's face lit up when he saw who was assigned to hear his case. It was Judge Hal Artest. He knew him very well. Judge Artest looked directly at Geno as he took his seat behind the bench.

Judge Artest wore the look of a man who had his arch nemesis right where he wanted him to administer a sweet dose of karma. His disdain for Geno was almost on the same level as the hatred Mayhem harbored in his heart for him. Judge Artest despised the way Geno manipulated the legal system in his favor to get defendants he knew were guilty of vicious crimes acquitted of all of the charges levied against them. He hated his cockiness and the way he flaunted his wealth before the public. For Geno's fate to be in the hands of a Judge who despised his very existence didn't bode too well for him. Judge Artest took his place behind the bench and called the courtroom to order. The idle chatter from the onlookers and press ceased instantly.

"Mr. Caprese, I would say it was good to see you, but given the circumstances, that wouldn't be appropriate. You are being accused of some very serious crimes here. I must say I am extremely disappointed to see you in my courtroom as a defendant since, as an attorney, you took an oath to uphold the law. Nonetheless, I'll reserve judgment until the facts are presented. Mr. Mayhem, are you ready to proceed?" Judge Artest asked stoically.

Geno wanted to walk up to the bench and slap the Judge for talking to him in such a manner. He had no right to judge him. His hands were just as dirty as Geno's were. He had a folder filled with some of his underhanded deeds stashed away as well.

"I am, your Honor. Mr. Caprese is being accused of ten counts of federal income tax evasion and filing false income tax returns. We believe that, with willful intent, Mr. Caprese has attempted to launder over fifty million dollars in undocumented income through a local banking institution by creating fictitious corporations to filter the money into offshore accounts. We have a wealth of incriminating evidence and a witness who will corroborate our allegations, your Honor. Because of the seriousness of these charges, the Government is requesting that Mr. Caprese be denied bail and be held over for trial. We believe he is a serious flight risk. Mr. Caprese has a wealth of resources at his disposal to be able disappear without a trace so

that he won't have to face the music for his crimes,"
Mayhem argued.

"Judge Artest, I believe that the prosecutor is
stretching the truth quite a bit with his assertions.
Mr. Mayhem has a long standing vendetta against
Mr. Caprese for personal reasons which he is using
this court's time to carry out. However, my client is
a well respected attorney with strong ties to the
community. He has never been convicted of a crime
in his entire life. He has a beautiful wife and two
loving children. He has no reason to flee the
country because he is innocent of these charges. He
plans to stand and face these false allegations that
have been leveled against him. Therefore, we
believe that the request to deny him bail would be
unjust and a violation of his civil liberties. We ask
that a reasonable bond be set for Mr. Caprese,"
Solomon rebutted. He sat back in his seat. Geno
patted him on the shoulder for what he perceived
to be a job well done.

"You both make compelling arguments and I
am torn as to what to decide. While I agree that
Mr. Caprese has strong ties to the community, I can
also see why he might be a flight risk given the
circumstances. Geno, you are being accused of
hiding a lot of money from the federal government.
I think you, of all people, know what kind of jail
time you are facing if you're convicted. Looking at
that fact alone is enough of a reason for any man

to go on the lam. As for you, Mr. Price, I don't know anything about any personal issues between Mr. Caprese and the prosecutor nor do I care. If it doesn't relate to a legal argument, then I am not concerned with those matters. That is something they need to hash out between themselves at a later date. To err on the side of caution, I am going to revisit the issue of bail at a later date and recommend that the defendant remain in custody for the time being," Judge Artest stated firmly.

Geno had a stunned look on his face. He was furious. He jumped up from his seat to speak. Solomon tried to stop him, but he was too late. He was compelled to speak his mind before the court today and nothing could deter him.

"Is this a joke? Judge Artest, you can't be serious! You're not going to let Mayhem get away with this, are you? Your Honor, I respectfully submit that these charges are bogus. Please reconsider the issue of bail at this time!" Geno pleaded with the court. He was totally out of character, but he didn't care. He had no intention of spending another night behind bars. The few days he already spent in custody were enough for him.

"Mr. Price, I ask at this time that you control your client! I will not tolerate anymore loud outbursts in my courtroom! Mr. Caprese, my decision has been made. Your attorney will have another opportunity to make a case for me to grant you bail. Until that time, you will just have to accept my decision as it stands. Bailiff, take Mr. Caprese into custody," the Judge ordered.

While he did his best to maintain a professional demeanor on the outside, Judge Artest took a bit of pleasure at the sight of Geno Caprese out of control as he pleaded for his freedom. He loved being in a position to be able to detain him in a jail cell even if it might be for a brief period of time. He felt it served Geno well to get a taste of his own medicine for once. Artest slyly glanced in Mayhem's direction and gave him a subtle nod of approval.

Geno noticed the interaction between them and made a mental note. There were loud rumblings among the court spectators. Some were upset Geno had to remain behind bars, while others cheered the Judge's decision. Solomon did his best to assure him he would get him out on bail. Even though Solomon was a competent attorney, he didn't have what it took to get the job done alone in this situation. It would take more than his ability to litigate effectively in the courtroom to get Geno off on these charges.

Solomon had yet to learn the art of playing high stakes chess with social power brokers like Mayhem and Artest. He wasn't privy to the knowledge of how most real power moves in society were made. They didn't take place in the public, but behind closed doors as a result of skillful maneuvering and strategic planning on another level. These were things Geno planned to teach him over time, but for now, those lessons would have to wait.

Mayhem had Geno boxed in, but Geno was determined to fight his way out of his predicament. Geno knew what needed to be done if he wanted to get back on the streets where he could be most effective in helping Solomon beat the case. Before he was escorted out of the courtroom, he whispered explicit directions into Solomon's ear for him to follow. Once he was clear he understood his instructions, he turned toward the guards and was escorted out of the courtroom. The news reporters jumped out of their seat quickly to get a statement from him. Geno gave them nothing. He had no witty response for them to quote.

Carina's eyes filled up with tears as she watched Geno being taken away. The way things stood, it would at least be a few more restless nights before Geno had a chance to come home to her and the children. That was a few days too many for her. The more days he spent behind bars, the more it began to sink in Carina's head Geno might be gone away from his family for a long time if Mayhem had his way. Carina wasn't ready to face life without Geno in the picture. Sal and Cesare did their best to comfort and console her. Solomon gathered up his belongings and headed out of the courtroom. He had his work cut out for him.

Chapter 5

The last place Cesare wanted to be today was at work, but he knew even in Geno's absence, the show had to go on. He sat behind his desk in his office at the Foundation reviewing some paperwork related to a new game he and Jeremy had in the works. He got into the office at around seven in the morning because he couldn't sleep. He popped two Ibuprofen pills in his mouth and took a sip from his glass of water to try and quell his massive headache. He also tried to ease the pain by massaging his temples, but that didn't work either. He was stressed out and angry. He got up from his desk, turned around, and punched the wall in an attempt to release his rage. Instead, he made things worse because not only was he frustrated, but now he might have a broken hand to boot. He yelled out loud from the excruciating pain he was in. He felt foolish after he realized what he had done.

"Cesare, are you okay?" Jeremy asked frantically from the doorway. He was in his office when he heard the loud sound and ran down the hall to see what was going on.

"I'm fine, Jeremy. I don't feel like being bothered right now. Close the door behind you," Cesare barked at him. He knew he was wrong to talk to Jeremy in such a disrespectful manner, but he didn't care. He needed somebody to vent his anger at, and Jeremy was the closest target.

"You're not okay, Cesare. That hand might be broken. We need to get you to a hospital," Jeremy tried to reason with him.

He didn't take Cesare's harsh tone personal because he understood the source of his frustration. He too was upset about Geno's arrest because he felt indebted to him as well. When Geno purchased his company from him, he changed Jeremy's life for the better. Ever since they formed a business partnership, life had been uphill for him and he owed it all to Geno's shrewd business guidance and influence. He was the best mentor any struggling entrepreneur could ever hope to have. Because of Geno, he was no longer a talented computer geek with infinite potential, but he was now a key player in one of the most well respected corporations in the worldwide video gaming community.

"I said I'm fine. Now just let me be!" Cesare reiterated with just as much venom in his tone.

"Have it your way, my friend. I'm here if you need me," Jeremy replied. He saw that his attempt to help Cesare fell upon deaf ears. Jeremy decided to take Cesare's advice and exit his office. As he was about to leave, he was startled when he saw Jericho walking toward him. His dark, mysterious aura terrified Jeremy. He simply spoke and got away from him as fast as he could.

"Are you ok? What the hell did you do to your hand?" Jericho asked. He noticed him rubbing it to try and soothe away the pain.

"I was pissed off. I accidentally banged it on the wall," he replied. Cesare knew better than to respond disrespectfully to Jericho like he just did to Jeremy. Jericho's response wouldn't be as a cordial to say the least.

"You better put some ice on that before it swells up. You said you wanted to meet up so we can talk. You got me up out of my bed at the crack of dawn, so what's up?"

"This motherfucker Sam Bradford needs to die for snitching on Geno. We need to make him disappear," Cesare replied angrily.

"I can make that happen. All I need is a location and it's a done deal," Jericho stated nonchalantly. He was surprised to hear Cesare talk in such a manner. He never saw this aggressive to side him.

"We can reach out to Geno's detective guy, John Lucci. I'm sure he'll be able to find him," he suggested.

"Okay, you handle that part and I'll do the rest. For now, let's take care of that hand, tough guy," Jericho suggested in a joking manner.

Cesare tried his best to allow for work to be a distraction from dealing with the fact Geno, his big brother and father figure, faced a long prison sentence if he was convicted of the charges he faced. For as long as he could remember, he viewed Geno as invincible and untouchable by the law. No matter what the problem was, Geno always had the right solution to make the problem go away. He could never remember a situation where Geno didn't have the upper hand on his opponent. However, Geno clearly was blindsided with this situation.

Never would Cesare have imagined Sam would become a snitch. With all of the love Geno showed all of his business partners and employees, it was a tough pill to swallow that Sam would turn against him. Geno put himself on the line for anybody he considered as a member of his immediate or extended family. There wasn't a problem he wouldn't try to fix for a friend if it were in his power to do so.

Being honest, Cesare never cared for Sam ever since the day he voted against him becoming a board member. Now with his betrayal of Geno, Cesare had more of a reason to hate him with every fiber of his being. Because of his weak character and inability to accept responsibility for his own legal situation like a stand up guy should do, Geno's freedom was now on the line. How to make Sam pay for being a turncoat was all that crossed his mind. Geno needed his help and he planned to do whatever he could to assist him. Despite all of the ups and downs in their relationship throughout the years, Geno was always there for him when it counted the most. He got him out of more than enough sticky situations and now it was Cesare's chance to return the favor. With Sam under federal protection, it would be almost impossible to get to him, but he was determined to find a way. He had never killed anyone before, but he was willing to make an exception in this instance.

Cesare knew Geno needed help and that was why he reached out to Jericho and John Lucci for assistance. They were the perfect partners in crime to have in this situation. Lucci had connections in law enforcement on all levels and if anybody could find a way to get access to where the Feds were hiding Sam at, it would be him. Once they found Sam, he would need Jericho's expertise as an assassin to find a way to eliminate him before he had a chance to testify in court against Geno. He didn't have a lot of time to put his plan in motion.

He needed to act quickly. For now, he left the office with Jericho to go to the emergency room to get his hand checked out.

Chapter 6

Ever since his twin brother Jarvis' brutal murder at the hands of Nesta's henchmen, Milton Jackson fell into a state of deep depression. It was hard for him to cope with life without Jarvis being around. For as long as he could remember, they did everything together from partying to selling drugs to opening up multiple businesses together. Now that Jarvis was gone, it was as though a part of Milton died with him. He had recurring dreams about the last face to face conversation they had. The images of Jarvis he saw in his dreams were very vivid and so real they gave him a false sense of hope his brother was still alive. However, once he woke up out of his sleep, he was forced to face the grim reality they would never see each other again in this lifetime.

All of the plans they made to grow old together as wealthy tycoons who raised their children to be as thick as thieves like they were had been crushed.

He blamed his brother's death on Geno. In his mind, Jarvis would still be alive if he didn't get caught up in the crossfire of Geno's war with Nesta. His blood was on his hands. When he saw Geno, he acted like their relationship was the same, but deep down inside, Milton hated the sight of his face. He wanted him to feel the same pain he felt to have lost his brother. He had to place the blame on someone for his sorrow. Geno made for as good a target as anyone else.

Milton isolated himself from most of his inner circle. Days would pass by with him not leaving out of his spacious mansion. He didn't want to talk to anybody. He left Moreno in charge of running things for him while he spent his time wallowing in his misery. Moreno jumped at the opportunity to be in charge. He was a young hungry bull who was eager to show Milton he could handle more responsibility. He stepped up like a true soldier and kept things afloat for Milton while he went through this rough patch in his life.

Currently, Milton was sprawled across the couch in his living room area dressed in a pair of boxers, a wife beater t-shirt, and a full length robe. His normally well kept house reeked of funk from his body odor because he hadn't showered in three days. He was surrounded by debris and trash from the empty bottles of alcohol and takeout food he had consumed over the past few days. He had put on at least ten pounds of fat onto his usually athletic and toned physique. Going to the gym to exercise was the furthest thing from his mind right now. He just wanted the days to pass him by until he found a way to ease the pain he felt. Every day was a battle with himself for his sanity.

With the remote control in his hand, he turned on the flat screen TV and the DVD player. For hours on end, he watched home videos he and Jarvis had made over the years of the epic parties they held at various locations. Images of them popping bottles of champagne and entertaining hordes of beautiful women flashed across the TV screen and briefly brought a smile to his face. That smile would be replaced shortly by feelings of anger directed at one person, Geno Caprese. When he lost Jarvis, he lost more than his brother. He lost his best friend.

Milton began to wonder why Geno always seemed to end up unscathed by the violence that came along with the lifestyle they led. He never caught one bullet in return for all of the murders he ordered. Even though Geno offered his condolences for his loss, that wasn't enough to satisfy Milton. He needed to know what it felt like to lose someone you love. He no longer viewed Geno as a brother, friend, and business partner. He had now become his enemy and someone he hoped to exact revenge upon for his brother's death. While in a drunken state, he had many visions of killing Geno in a vicious manner. However, for now, he kept his feelings to himself.

Milton was interrupted out of his pity party by a knock at his front door. He took another sip from the nearly empty bottle of liquor situated in front of him. He didn't bother to get up to answer the door because he knew who it was. It was Moreno. He stopped by twice a week to give him an update on their business dealings. When Milton didn't answer the door, Moreno let himself in with the spare key he left under a flower pot in the front of his house. Moreno walked into the room where Milton was at and became repulsed by the awful smell in the room and Milton's rugged appearance. He wasn't used to seeing him like this. The Milton he knew was always on point and serious about his business. The man in front of him looked just the opposite. He had to let his feelings about Milton's current state of mind be known.

"Damn cuz, you look like shit. What the hell is the matter with you? You need to get your shit together. It ain't like you to let the world get you down," Moreno stated directly. He was used to the image of Milton dressed in a suit and imparting wisdom onto him about saving money and planning for the future. It hurt him to see Milton looking like a crusty and haggardly fat old man who should be out on a street corner somewhere begging for loose change.

"Shut up, Mo, you know what's going on with me. I lost my fucking brother. I'm fucked up in the head right now. I can't think straight. Are you saying you don't miss Jarvis?" he asked. He took his hand and picked at his teeth to remove the remnants of the pizza from the night before that was stuck between them.

"Stop talking crazy, Milton. You know I miss my big cuz. We are all family. Just like you, he was more like a brother to me, but you know I don't get caught up in all of that emotional shit. Dying comes with the game. No matter what happens out in the streets, I gotta keep it moving. I gotta stay sharp before I get caught slipping," he replied. Moreno spoke like a true veteran of the street life. He lived and died by the G code that his big cousins taught him. It seemed as though Milton needed a reminder of how things should be.

"I know you're right. I just need some time to get my head right. Thanks for stepping up for me, Mo. What do you have in that bag?" he asked.

"Aaaahhhh, I'm glad you asked me that question. You know I ain't come here empty handed," Moreno replied.

He handed Milton the heavy duffle bag he brought with him. It contained close to two hundred grand inside from the week's drug proceeds. When Milton opened it up and looked inside, his face lit up for a brief moment.

"Now, this right here is what I'm talking about! It's something about the sight of money that can make everything bad around me not matter at least for a moment," Milton declared. To see Moreno able to generate this much money in a week let him know their drug spots were still running smoothly without him having to lift a finger.

"Exactly, cuz, and that's why I need you back on your A game so we can do this together. Jarvis wouldn't want you hanging your head down. Big cuz is probably looking down from heaven saying y'all better not be wasting time crying over me when it's money out in these streets to be made," he joked. Milton knew he was right. He could hear his brother saying those exact words. Jarvis was a true hustler at heart. He never let a dollar slip through his hands.

"I'm glad you stopped by. I needed this little rap session. I'ma get it together real soon."

Even though Moreno's words struck a chord with him, Milton was still stuck in his current state of denial about his drinking problem. He had no intention of putting the bottle down. It had become his best friend and soul source of comfort. Nothing else allowed him to have a moment of relief to be able to temporarily forget about his brother's death. In fact, as soon as Moreno left his house, he planned to fix himself a stiff drink and continue to drown himself in his misery.

"So, what do you think about this whole situation with Geno getting knocked off for income tax evasion? The Feds are not playing. They're trying to give him football numbers."

"That's his problem not mine. As long as my name ain't on them indictment papers, I ain't worried. Shit, I lost my brother over his beef. Let him take the heat for this one on his own. Geno ain't never done a day in jail in his life while we stood by his side in every war he ever had in these streets. We took those hits on the front line, not him. Besides, if he goes down, it's more money in the pot for us to go get," Milton replied without a hint of concern in his voice for someone he once pledged to ride or die with for life. Moreno was surprised by his response. He thought Milton and Geno were like family, but clearly something had changed between them. Death had a way of driving a wedge between men.

"Oh, it's like that now? Say no more, cuz. You know I ride with you until the end. We're bound by this blood thing and that ain't gonna change for nothing," Moreno stated to reaffirm his allegiance to Milton. If Milton had an issue with Geno, then so did he. Moreno was just happy to see Milton start to get a little bounce back in his step. Now they could get back to what was important: the money. Anything else was just a distraction.

Chapter 7

Sal was in a bad mood today. If he had his way, he would find Sam Bradford and kill him with his bare hands. He would love to strangle him until he saw the last breath of air exit out of his lungs. He wanted to rip out his tongue so there was no way he could use it to testify and put Geno behind bars. His anger was not so much about Geno; it was more so his contempt for men who disrespected the street code of silence.

Sal had no problem getting his hands dirty especially in situations like this. Even though he bought into Geno's idea of building a legitimate business empire, Sal was a gangster to the core. He was taught to live by a code of honor because without rules to the game, there would be no order in the underworld. Without order, chaos would rule in the streets and that would be bad for business for everybody involved. In an atmosphere of chaos, nobody could eat. Sal was raised to live by the street code of never snitching to the police about illegal activities. He would give his life or do life in jail before he violated this golden rule. Even though Sam wasn't from the streets like he and Geno were, he still benefitted from their dirty money and thus had to be held to the same code of conduct. He was just as guilty as they were by association.

With Geno out of commission, Sal was Geno's top underboss and he took it upon himself to take charge of the daily operations of the Foundation. He felt he was more than prepared to do the job in his absence. He paid close attention to every lesson Geno taught him about the multiple levels of the organizational structure of the Foundation. He put in many long hours at the office shadowing the heads of each business entity under the company's umbrella so he could have hands on experience about their day to day operations. Even though he lacked the academic credentials to be a business executive, he more than made up for it with his sharp mind and street smarts. What colleges taught in four years, he learned on the job under the tutelage of a shrewd man like Geno.

Sal also saw this as his moment to shine. It didn't sit too well with Sal that Geno gave more responsibility recently to Cesare and mentioned his intentions to do the same for his long lost brother, Jericho, in the near future. He felt some kind of way about Geno's plans because he didn't believe they put in the amount of work he did to earn his spot as a top dog in the Foundation. He was particularly leery of Jericho after Geno made it known about Jericho's initial plans to kill him. It wasn't like Geno to let something like this slide as though it were insignificant.

Coming from the streets, Sal knew if a person wanted you dead one day, but changed his mind for some particular reason, there was nothing stopping that individual from having the same ill intentions for you in the future. To add insult to injury, Geno barely knew him but still chose to put Jericho in charge of security so quickly. He never said a thing to Geno about his choice even though he felt he made such a decision in haste and out of guilt because of the way his father treated Jericho and Shavon for so many years. The Geno he knew never made decisions based upon his emotions. He generally acted off of his intellect and superior wisdom as opposed to just his gut feelings. Sal knew how important family was to Geno, but he also felt Jericho should have to do more to earn a spot in the Caprese family. He put in a ton of work to become an underboss and he believed Jericho should do the same. Sal kept a close eye on Jericho every time he was around him because he flat out did not trust him. Jericho never did anything in particular to make him feel that way about him. One could argue Sal felt threatened by his presence. His own insecurity and paranoia made him dislike Jericho.

Geno never said or did anything to make him believe he would replace him as his second in command with either Cesare or Jericho, but Sal was being proactive so he could solidify his position in the Foundation. He didn't want to give him a reason to ever not consider him as a top asset to the organization. There was no way in hell he would let two young cats like Cesare and Jericho sit in his seat. Despite his strong feelings about the situation for quite some time, Sal kept them to himself. He saw no reason to rock the boat unless it was absolutely necessary. For now, he just did his part and continued to mentor Cesare as Geno requested for him to do.

The fallout from Geno's arrest for financial misconduct would definitely have a negative impact on the business relationships he had worked so hard to build with all of the corporation's business partners. The Caprese Foundation's image took a beating in the press with stories being run that called into question Geno's business dealings with alleged organized crime figures like the Jackson brothers. The stories questioned how he was able to acquire so much wealth so fast. They alleged that the Foundation was nothing more than a criminal outfit being run by gangsters who used illegal money to fund their legal businesses.

Even though all of the rumors were true, Geno, or any other board member for that matter, had yet to be convicted of any criminal activities. They were all being tried in the press and the court of public opinion. The negative storylines had many of his high profile business partners a little antsy and on edge because when it came to big business, nobody wanted to be associated with a scandal that could be detrimental to the significant profit margins Geno had always delivered on their investments.

All of the Foundation's investors needed to be reassured their business interests would be protected should Geno wind up being found guilty of the charges he faced and had to serve major prison time. Geno had built a good rapport with all of them to show he was fully capable of doing the job of making all of these rich men richer. He talked a good game to get them to invest their money in the Foundation and delivered on what he promised them. The Caprese brand was certified as a tried and true commodity. It was Sal's job to make sure it stayed that way. With Geno potentially out of the picture for a good minute, Sal had to step up to reassure them all that the Foundation was still on solid ground. This was the reason Sal called the emergency meeting he had scheduled for today.

The Foundation's other board members and its various business investors entered the meeting room at the Caprese Foundation's headquarters one by one. Sal stood at the door to greet them all individually. He shook each and every one of their hands with a firm grip and accompanied his handshake with a confident smile. One of the greatest business lessons he learned from Geno was the importance of projecting an aura of confidence even in times of adversity. Being a winner was a twenty-four hour job and required the ability to be able to see the light at the end of the tunnel even in the dimmest of situations.

The press beat up on the Caprese Foundation daily, but it didn't matter. The organization was still a winner in the most important area and that was it still had the ability to generate maximum financial returns from its investments. Profit margins remained just as stable as they were before Geno's arrest. Images on the television screen of armed federal agents storming into the office of the Foundation to seize documents and computers only served to create more interest from the general public. People wanted to know if Geno was as powerful as he was rumored to be. Geno developed a cult like following among the common everyday working people. The socially disadvantaged loved to see someone challenge the status quo of the wealthy upper class or to beat a government it considered to be corrupt system at its own game.

This moment would prove to be a pivotal one in the Foundation's ability to remain a powerhouse in corporate America. The stakes were high, but he was up for the task. If Sal failed to instill confidence in their investors, Geno would be gravely disappointed in him. To come up short would have grave repercussions he had no intentions of facing. He had to come up big in convincing the Foundation's investors not to pull their money out of the organization.

When Milton Jackson arrived, he was accompanied by Moreno. Sal noticed his physical appearance was out of the ordinary. He wasn't dressed in his usual business suit, but had on a pair of jeans and a Polo shirt. They both were wrinkled like he had slept in his clothes the night before. His beard was scraggly and he smelled like a brewery. As one of the top leaders of the Foundation, this was the wrong image their investors needed to see at this crucial time. Sal understood the fact he recently lost his brother, but that was no excuse for him to show up at a business meeting looking like a train wreck. When he shook his hand, Sal walked him out of the board room to have a conversation. There was no way he could let him sit in an important meeting like this one being drunk.

"Milton, what the hell is wrong with you? Do you understand what's going on here today?" Sal inquired.

"Sal, what's up, Cat Daddy? Yeah, it's messed up how they're trying to do my boy, Geno. That ain't right. It's a damn shame," he uttered.

"I know you're going through some personal shit, but this is unacceptable. How the hell can you show up to a business meeting wasted? You look like a hobo. You need to go home and sober up. We can talk about this tomorrow. Moreno, take him back home please before he embarrasses us in front of all of these important people," Sal advised him.

"They're important people? Oh, I'm not important? I ain't going no damn where. I got a right to be here just like you, Sal," he stated angrily. He leaned forward and almost fell over when he tried to poke Sal in the chest with his finger. Sal's first instinct was to gut punch Milton for his disrespect, but he opted against that idea. He didn't want to cause a scene. That was the last thing he needed right now.

"Come, on, Milton. I told you this was a bad idea. Let's get out of here," Moreno said. He wrapped Milton's arm around his shoulders and forcefully walked him toward the elevator. Milton mumbled a host of profane words at Sal the entire time. Sal took note of every word and planned to address his disrespect at a later date.

Milton's drunken state didn't go unnoticed by some of the men who walked past him and Moreno on their way to the elevator. They shook their heads in disgust and covered their noses to block out the cloud of funk that followed Milton. It was an embarrassing scene to say the least. Sal had his work cut out for him to clean up this mess. Cesare and Jericho were getting off of the elevator just as Milton and Moreno were making their exit. Cesare was about to speak to Milton, but once he saw he was in bad shape, he just kept on walking past him. He nodded his head to acknowledge Moreno, who appeared to be at a loss for words to explain Milton's current state. When Cesare and Jericho were about to enter the meeting room, Sal reached out his arm and stopped Jericho in his tracks. Jericho looked down at Sal's arm as it made contact with his chest. His first instinct was to snap his neck for violating his person, but Cesare sensed his anger and intervened before he had a chance to react.

"Sal, what's the problem?" Cesare interjected. He looked at Jericho and back at Sal. They both glared at each other like two pit bulls about to go at it in a dog cage.

"Jericho, my man, this meeting is for business partners only. You'll have to wait outside," Sal stated coldly. The eye contact between them remained intense.

"Sal, Jericho is family. He has every right to be here. What are you doing?" Cesare inquired.

"Jericho is head of security, Cesare. This meeting is for business partners only. I don't have time to argue about this. Let's get this meeting started. We have work to do," Sal replied.

"This is bullshit, Sal, and you know it is."

Cesare was not happy at all, but was powerless to do anything to change the situation. Sal was Geno's right hand man. When Geno wasn't around, he was in charge and Cesare had to respect this fact. He didn't understand Sal's issue with Jericho nor did he care. He had love for Sal, but Jericho was his blood brother. His first line of loyalty was with family.

"It's all good, Cesare. Go ahead and handle your business. I know my place. I'll be in my office. Call me when you're done," Jericho butted in.

He looked Sal up and down and smirked. He sensed Sal never liked him from the first time they met, but he didn't care. He never said a word to Geno or Cesare about the issue, but kept it to himself. One of the tricks of the trade he mastered was the art of being patient. When the time was right, he and Sal would have a chance to dance. Jericho had just the right remedy to address whatever issues Sal had with him. Cesare walked into the meeting and Sal followed behind him. He made sure he closed the door behind him directly in Jericho's face. Jericho simply smiled and walked away.

Sal yelled into the microphone in an attempt to quiet down the chatter in the room. It took a few minutes before everyone heeded his instructions and ended their sidebar conversations. He had an audience of about fifty individuals in front of him of all nationalities and races. Geno wisely chose a group of financial investors that represented the demographic makeup of America. He wanted every ethnic group and race to be represented within the Foundation. He envisioned it was this inclusiveness which would help to legitimize the Foundation's image to the world as a reflection of the American dream whereby all people have an equal chance to achieve financial success. It was a brilliant idea on his part as it had worked up until this point in the Foundation's history.

"I would like to first of all apologize for inconveniencing you all by having you attend a meeting on the weekend on such short notice. However, time is of the essence as this is a crucial matter. With the recent arrest of our CEO and founder, Geno Caprese, I know you all may have some concerns about your business interests here at the Caprese Foundation. I would like to first state that the charges that have been leveled against Mr. Caprese are absolutely false and we plan to fight them vigorously with every resource at our disposal. Mr. Caprese is the victim of a vicious federal prosecutor who has a personal axe to grind with

him, but his efforts will not prevail. He is also the victim of one wayward board member who we can clearly see is not here today. As it turns out, he chose to break the law and wound up getting caught. In an effort to get himself out of his situation, he dragged Mr. Caprese into the fray. It should also be noted that Geno's legal issues are an attack on his personal finances and not the organization. You can rest assured that your money is safe here at the Foundation. In Mr. Geno's absence, I will make myself available to address any questions any of you may have as a group or individually to ease your anxiety. The reality of this entire ordeal is the Caprese Foundation has been and will continue to be an upstanding corporation that has operated above board with you all in the most ethical and professional manner. At this time I would like to open the floor to answer any questions you may have."

Sal spoke eloquently to his captive audience. His speech was clearly well received. Sal took the time to answer each and every question with elaborate detail. For the most part, the Foundation's business partners seemed to be impressed with his presentation and walked away from the meeting reassured that their money was in good hands. After they all had a chance to converse amongst themselves for a few minutes, everyone departed from the room seemingly happy. Calm had been restored at the Caprese Foundation for now. How long that would last depended on the outcome of Geno's legal situation.

Chapter 8

"Damn, that hurt!" Geno yelled in pain as he grabbed his arm. He just finished up his morning ritual of doing five hundred crunches and two hundred and fifty pushups. On the last pushup he completed, he accidentally jerked his arm and sensed he may have pulled or strained a muscle. He grabbed a towel off of his bunk and wiped the beads of sweat from his brow. Exercising served as a way for Geno to take his mind off of the fact he was still locked up. He needed something to take his mind away from the grimness of his current situation.

"Is everything okay, OG?," Remy, his young cellmate, asked.

In his early twenties, Remy, whose full name was Raimondo Ruggiero, was locked up for credit card fraud. He was being held over for trial because he couldn't afford to pay the fifty thousand dollar bail that was set for him. When he found out his cellmate was the infamous Geno Caprese, he damn near lost his mind. He grew up in Geno's old neighborhood in Little Italy and knew all about the legendary Caprese boys. His father, Angelo, used to run with Silvio back in the day when he first got into chopping down stolen cars. Remy was awe struck to be in Geno's presence. He made his admiration known from the moment they met. He went out of his way to show the proper respect and adulation a Boss like Geno deserved.

"It's all good, Remy. You know when you reach the age of forty, your body doesn't respond the way it used to do when I was a young bull like you," Geno joked, but he was dead serious. Geno was in excellent physical condition because he worked out several times a week, but no man escaped the fate of Father time when the aches and pains from the wear and tear on the joints and tendons of the human body decided to kick in. He could use a nice full body massage right now, but being in jail, that wasn't going to happen. He would just have to tough it out until the pain subsided.

"You're not old, Geno. You can sell that line to somebody else. Not many of these young dudes in here are cut up like you are. My Pops used to tell me about how you used to knock fools out back in the old neighborhood," Remy reminisced on the many stories his father shared with him about Geno's boxing skills when they were younger. His father died a few years ago from a stroke while he was incarcerated.

"Your father was a good man, Remy. He was a stand up guy. Every time he went inside, he kept his mouth shut and did his time like a man. He stayed true to this thing of ours. I hope you do the same with your crew. It's too many rodents running around today out in these streets. They all need to be exterminated. There is no more honor amongst wise guys today," Geno argued.

Being on the other side of the law as an attorney, he saw too many guys he knew from the old neighborhood who he thought were street soldiers turn into informants once they got put in a jail cell. Every man is not built to withstand the harsh reality of everyday jail life. That was why Geno would always advise his clients he saw as being a little soft to change their way of life before they did the dishonorable thing of becoming a snitch to avoid going to jail.

"You don't have to worry about me, Geno. My Daddy raised me right. I hate them cats that eat the cheese too," Remy stated boldly.

Geno cracked up laughing at his choice of words. His little rap sessions with Remy served as a brief moment of escape from the frustration of everyday jail life. It had been almost two weeks since his initial court appearance and he wanted out of this hell hole. He felt trapped mentally and physically. He just needed Solomon to come through for him as expected.

"So, what's the deal with your case? How much is your bail?" Geno inquired.

"They got me in here for using stolen credit cards. I had a girl who worked for American Express who was in on the scam with me. She would give me a list of client account numbers and I would use them to purchase high end purses, clothes, and shoes which I would resell on the streets for less than the store price. It was easy money until we got caught. My bail is fifty thousand dollars, but I'm not stressing over that because I know I'ma do some time due to this being my third charge," Remy replied. He had served almost four years total in jail in his life for other credit fraud charges as well as for marijuana possession. To do a bid was nothing new to him. He resolved himself to accept his fate for his crime.

"Is that all your bail amount is? Fifty grand is nothing. I'ma take care of that for you when I meet with my attorney later this week. You probably have a public defender, don't you?"

"Yeah, I do. That's all I can afford," Remy replied humbly.

"All hope is not loss, young blood. I'ma have one of my lawyers at my firm take a look at your case. We do a great amount of pro bono work every year. Don't give up hope just yet. A lot of times, things are not as bad as you may think they are."

"You would do that for me? I don't know what to say but thanks Geno. I owe you big time for this," Remy replied. His pessimistic outlook on life was now more optimistic.

"You don't owe me a damn thing. You're from the old neighborhood. You're family. I take care of my own. When you get out of here, I'ma get you a real job so you can be a real earner and not have to get caught up with penny-ante credit card schemes."

The look on Remy's face said it all. He was eternally grateful for Geno's gesture. He did his best to not get emotional because he didn't want Geno to think he was soft. Their conversation was cut short when another inmate appeared in the doorway of their cell. Geno didn't recognize the man and neither did Remy. Normally, when a stranger came looking for you in the joint, it was never for a good reason. He either came to kill you or shake you down for something.

"Excuse me, homes, are you Geno Caprese?" the young inmate asked as he glanced in Geno's direction. His muscular arms were covered in tattoos that symbolized his gang affiliation.

"Who wants to know?" Remy barked back at him aggressively. He reached his hand behind his bunk to grab his shank. He got up and began to walk toward him. The man backed up and raised his hands in the air as a sign of surrender.

"Be easy, homes. I come in peace. I came to talk with Mr. Caprese in private. I've got some information for him from a mutual friend of ours," he insisted.

"Relax, Remy, I'm good. Step outside for a second so I can hear what the gentleman has to say," Geno stated calmly.

Geno was curious to know what information the man had for him. Even though he didn't recognize the man's face as someone he had saw before, he wasn't concerned about him doing him any harm. Geno was lethal with his hands and was more than qualified to defend himself. Remy did as Geno instructed and stepped out of the cell. The other inmate came inside to relay the message he had for Geno. When he was done conveying the information to Geno, he went on about his way. Whatever he told Geno livened up his mood. He was pumped up; he got back down on the cell floor and proceeded to do another set of pushups even though his arm was still sore.

Chapter 9

The calmness of the fall season had always been the most relaxing time of year for Jericho. He loved it when the temperature wasn't scorching hot or cold as ice, but somewhere in between. As he drove down the road in his brand new Chevrolet Suburban, he rolled his window down slightly to enjoy the slight breeze. Nina was in the passenger seat next to him tinkering with the radio. They were on their way to her prenatal doctor's appointment. Neither one of them could believe she was pregnant with their first child. However, Nina was almost five months along and her protruding belly was all the proof they needed to serve as confirmation they would soon be parents to a wonderful little bundle of joy.

When she found out she was pregnant, Nina was ecstatic. The first person she told was Shavon. She was equally as excited to have a little niece or nephew to spoil. Even though she was currently away at school, she planned to be home for the birth of her big brother's first child. Nothing brought Nina more joy than to be able to have a child with the man she loved. Jericho, however, was another story. Initially, he felt the timing wasn't right for them to start a family. He had just started working for Geno and he wanted to at least get comfortable with his new lifestyle before they took that step.

Over time, he warmed up to the idea of being a father. He hoped the baby was a boy, but would love his child just as much if it turned out to be a girl. He wanted nothing more than to be the father figure in his child's life that Leonardo never was to him. Being responsible for the care of his own child gave him a new sense of purpose for his life. For the bulk of his adult life, his every action was dedicated to causing death. Now he was focused on creating a peaceful life for his child. He noticed the growth and change in himself that took place on a daily basis. He was becoming the kind of man his mother would be proud to call her son.

"Woman, will you leave that radio alone Nina? You're starting to give me a headache the way you keep flipping those channels," he stated.

"You need to stop being grumpy, Mister. Ooohhhh, this is my jam!" she declared when she heard Alessa Cara's latest single come on. She turned up the volume and proceeded to dance in tune with the beat. Jericho simply shook his head and laughed at her horrible singing. She sounded like a dying animal on its last breath, but he sucked it up like a champ. For better or worse, Nina was the love of his life even if her singing did damage to his eardrums.

"Man, I'm glad we're finally here. Your singing got my ears aching," Jericho joked. Nina playfully punched him on his arm.

His eyes darted in the direction of the building the doctor's office was located in. He would soon escape from the screeching sound of Nina's horrible singing voice. He made a left turn at the traffic light and pulled into the parking lot. He parked the car, got out of his seat, and walked around to the passenger's side to help Nina climb down out of the truck. The expecting couple walked into the building and took the elevator up to the sixth floor. When they got off, they walked through the double doors into the lobby area. Nina signed in at the front desk and waited for the receptionist to call her name. To pass the time, Nina grabbed a copy of the latest issue of Essence magazine to read. Jericho busied himself surfing the web on his cell phone.

"Nina Devaughn, the doctor will see you now," the bubbly receptionist yelled out into the waiting area.

Jericho and Nina were led into the rear area by a nurse who took Nina's vital signs. She informed Nina that her readings were normal before she exited the room. After a brief wait, Dr. Lenora Rudolph appeared in the doorway to further examine her.

"Hello, Nina, how are things going? Mr. Jones, have you been making sure she's been getting her proper rest and taking her prenatal vitamins as prescribed?" Dr. Rudolph asked.

"My honey has been taking good care of me," Nina stated before Jericho had a chance to respond. He simply smiled and nodded his head in agreement.

"Nina, I need you to just lie back on the table so we can do an ultrasound to see how this little baby of yours is coming along," Dr. Rudolph instructed her.

Nina climbed up on the table and reclined back. She was full of nervous energy. Jericho held her hand to calm her down. Dr. Rudolph applied the cool gel on Nina's belly before she ran the scanning instrument across it several times in a swirling motion. The sound of the baby's heartbeat was like good music to both Nina and Jericho's ears. Dr. Rudolph carefully manipulated the instrument and observed the fetus' movements in the womb astutely.

"This is one beautiful little baby you have here. He seems to be growing perfectly. You can see his little hands and feet for yourself," Dr. Rudolph stated.

"Oh my goodness, did you just say HE? We're having a boy? Baby, did you hear that?" Nina stated. She was more than excited. She was overjoyed. She was glad the suspense not knowing her child's sex was over. Initially, they didn't want to know, but wound up changing their minds over time. Now Nina could properly shop for things to decorate the nursery. She visualized all of the cute baby items she could buy.

"Yes, you're having a boy," Dr. Rudolph confirmed.

"Look at my little man. He's gonna look just like me when he comes out," Jericho declared proudly. He was awe struck by the images he saw on the screen. To see his son's little hands and feet in their earliest stages was amazing. He felt a sense of joy like he never experienced before in his life. The emotional connection between him and his child was instant.

"Now, I just need you to take it easy and see me again in two weeks," Dr. Rudolph advised her. She wiped away the cooling gel from Nina's stomach. Nina got up from the table and straightened up her clothes before they made their exit.

While they walked back to the truck, Nina rambled on about all of the things she needed to get for their son's bedroom. Jericho acted as though he was listening to her, but his mind was elsewhere. It started to sink in he was about to be a father. He would be responsible for the care of a tiny little life that would be dependent on him and Nina for everything. It was really starting to ink in for him.

The whole ride home he thought about all of the things he wanted to do with his son like teaching him how to play basketball or taking him to get his first haircut. He thought about attending all of his graduation ceremonies. He planned to become the best father a little boy could ever hope to have. He never imagined himself having a family of his own, but he grew warm to the idea recently due to the positive chain of events that occurred in his life since he linked up with Geno. When they reached their home, he got out to open the door for Nina so she could go inside. He couldn't stay because he had business to tend to at the office. He gave Nina a kiss on the cheek and watched her go in the house before he pulled off.

Jericho drove less than three blocks from his house before he saw the flashing blue lights of a police car behind him. Reluctantly, he pulled over to the side of the road. He wasn't speeding and hadn't run a red light so he knew he hadn't done anything to break the law. This had to be another case where his crime was nothing more than being a young Black man who drove a high end truck with dark tinted windows. With the way police officers across the country were so callous and cold hearted in killing unarmed Black men for no justifiable reason, Jericho was determined to not become another victim. He unlocked the safety on the 9mm Glock he had positioned in between his seat and the center console. He was ready for battle if the cop tried to test his hand. When the officer reached his door, Jericho slowly rolled down his window.

"Jericho Jones, it's nice to finally meet you. I'm Homicide Detective Elvin Swift. I think we need to have an informal talk."

"How do you know my name? We don't have a damn thing to talk about. This is harassment. If you're not charging me with a crime Officer, you need to let me go on about my business," Jericho demanded. He was a little thrown off by the fact Swift knew his government name. He now knew his being pulled over had nothing to do with a traffic violation. This wasn't just a random case of racial profiling. His heart began to race. He firmly gripped his gun and was prepared to draw down on Swift, who sensed his anxiety.

"Take it easy, Jericho, you're not under arrest. I just want to talk to you about the murder of Marcus Harrison and your connection to Geno

Caprese," Swift stated to get right to the point. He had been monitoring Jericho's movements ever since he saw him with Geno at the hospital when they went to see their father right before he passed away.

"I work for Mr. Caprese as his head of security. Other than that, I don't have anything to say to you at all. I don't know anything about that man you just mentioned. I have never heard that name before in my life. If you have any more questions, you can talk to my lawyer," Jericho shot back defiantly. There was no way in hell he would walk into a police station voluntarily.

"That's your choice, playboy, if that's how you want to handle this matter. I guess your lawyer would be Geno Caprese himself, huh? I noticed you went to visit his father at the hospital and you were at his funeral. What's your relationship to Geno outside of working for him?" Swift asked.

"That's none of your business, Officer Swift, is it? Since I'm not under arrest, I'm about to pull off. You're making me nervous and when I get nervous, I don't think clearly," Jericho threatened him bluntly.

The fact Swift knew about his relationship with Geno indicated he had done some research on them but had not yet connected all of the dots together. He had no intention of providing him with any assistance with the matter either. He felt a rush of adrenaline flow through his body. He envisioned

Swift laid out in a pool of his own blood on the side of the road shortly if he didn't let him go on about his way. His trigger finger was getting itchy. Jericho had no fear whatsoever of law enforcement. Swift's fate hung in the balance as Jericho readied himself to take his life. The scene grew tenser by the second.

"Have it your way, Jericho. You will be hearing from me soon," Swift stated confidently as he walked back to his car.

Jericho breathed a sigh of relief. He waited until he was sure Detective Swift was gone before he decided to pull off. He thought for sure the Marcus Harrison murder was in the past, but clearly it wasn't. He wondered exactly what information Swift had in his possession to continue to hound him about the case. With Geno out of the picture, he couldn't rely on his resources to help him out this time. Jericho was on his own to deal with the situation. He was about to start a new chapter in his life with Nina and his new baby boy. There was no way in hell he would let Detective Swift put a damper on his plans.

Chapter 10

The Ronald Siebert Foundation's annual conference was an event that was very near and dear to Geno. The Foundation was named in honor of the son of a well-respected, but controversial Baltimore Circuit Court Judge, William Siebert. Ronald was diagnosed with bipolar disorder and depression at an early age. He was in and out of mental institutions for most of his adolescent years after several failed suicide attempts. Sadly, he took his own life at the age of twenty-one by jumping off of the Chesapeake Bay Bridge. After his tragic death, his father started the foundation to assist families in need of help in getting mental health treatment for their loved ones afflicted by mental illness. The Foundation targeted low income families who were most in need of the financial help. The Caprese Foundation was one of its largest donors every year.

Judge Seibert served as a mentor to Geno during his time in law school. Geno completed the bulk of his internship hours under his watchful eye. Judge Seibert grew up on the mean streets of Brooklyn, New York and he was drawn to the rough, edgy side he saw in Geno. The Judge was no stranger to controversy himself. He was widely rumored to be on the take, but was never formally charged or convicted of accepting bribes in exchange for judicial favors. It was his wealth of legal knowledge and willingness to bend the law in the interest of getting what he wanted that enabled him to forge such a strong bond with Geno. He broke down the ins and outs of the Maryland legal system to Geno in a way only he could after so many years of experience. He gave him a list of the biggest movers and shakers who wielded the most influence in the State and federal judicial systems. He taught Geno the art of conducting backdoor deals with judges without getting his hands dirty.

The two became the best of friends over the years. Geno owed a great deal of the power he now had to Judge Seibert's lessons. That was why after the Judge's death from a heart attack five years ago, Geno stepped up to the plate to become the largest contributor to the Foundation. It was the least he could do to continue the honorable efforts of his good friend.

Tonight happened to be the night of the Foundation's annual award ceremony which honored mental health organizations in the state of Maryland who played the most significant role in treating the disease of mental illness. The ceremony also served as a fundraising event to garner financial support from many of the Judge's colleagues in the legal system as well as his many wealthy philanthropist friends who chose to donate to the Judge's cause not out of sincere beneficence, but because their donations would serve as a significant tax break for them.

Geno was supposed to be in attendance at the conference, but was obviously unable to attend due to being incarcerated. Consequently, he sent Solomon in his place to represent the Caprese Foundation. He brought Geno's assistant, Jia, along as his date. Jia finally let go of her imaginary romance with Geno and decided to give Solomon a shot after he worked up the nerve to ask her out on a date two months ago. They clicked from that first night because they found out they had a great deal in common. They both were young and ambitious with a limitless future. They spent every moment they had away from the office together. When Geno found out about their relationship, he gave them his blessing. He thought they were good for one another and made a good couple.

"So, are you enjoying yourself?" Solomon leaned over and whispered to Jia. They had just finished up their meal and were relaxing listening to the music being played by the jazz band. It wasn't a Kendrick Lamar concert, but the laid back, mature vibe of the event allowed them a chance to broaden their cultural horizons by doing something different.

"Everything is nice. The atmosphere in here is really laid back. This is definitely a change in pace from what I'm used to seeing when I have went out on dates in the past," she answered. She was awestruck being in the company of so many rich and influential people. It was one of the perks that came along with being affiliated with Geno Caprese.

"Well, that's because you're in the presence of a real man. Those other guys you dated were little boys," Solomon teased her.

"Whatever, Solomon. No, for real, I'm glad you asked me to come with you to this event," Jia replied.

"I'm glad to hear you're having a good time. If you leave it up to me, we will have many more enjoyable nights like this. The sky's the limit for us. On another note, I need to use the restroom. I'll be right back in a few."

Solomon felt privileged to be able to start his law career under the watchful eye of such an accomplished attorney like Geno. He paid close attention to every detail of every lesson Geno imparted onto him. He was taken back when he got the call from Geno to be his attorney in this case because there were so many more experienced and qualified attorneys at the law firm who could have done the job. He didn't understand Geno's logic in choosing him to be his lawyer, but he had no intention of wasting the opportunity. He had to win this case for him. He saw this opportunity as a test for him from Geno. If he passed with flying colors, he believed Geno would appreciate his efforts and reward him properly with a chance to increase his salary and move him one step closer to becoming a partner in the law firm.

Conversely, if he failed to get Geno acquitted, his career hung in the balance because the one thing he learned about Geno was he hated to be let down or disappointed. Solomon had no intention of failing in his efforts. Geno not only sent him to the event to represent the Caprese Foundation, but he also sent him there to meet a person who could help him get Geno out of jail. As he scanned the room, he located the man he was sent to find. When he saw him headed toward the bathroom, Solomon saw this as the perfect moment for him to make his move. He got up from the table and followed closely behind the man. He was nervous, but he had to do what he had to. His boss sent him to do a job and he had to get it done. When he got close enough to the man, he tapped him on the shoulder. The man turned around, obviously startled. He had a very unhappy look on his face.

"Excuse me, Sir, are you Judge Bukowski?" Solomon asked.

"Yes, I am. Who are you young man?"

"Your honor, my name is Solomon Price. I'm an attorney. Can I have a moment of your time?" he replied.

"I'm headed to the can, son. Let's make this quick. What is it that you need?"

"Well, Sir, I was told to reach out to you by my boss, Geno Caprese. He told me to tell you that the bill you owe is now due. He sent me to collect his debt."

"Young man, are you sure you know what you're doing?" he asked. He wanted to be sure Solomon understood the gravity of the situation Geno got him involved with to approach him in such a manner.

"I'm absolutely sure I know what I'm doing," Solomon replied without batting an eye.

Judge Bukowski heard about Geno's arrest in the news. It was also the current hot topic in the local legal community. He felt it was a shame he was arrested because he always thought highly of Geno as an attorney, but he also knew Geno was probably guilty of the charges based upon the rumors he heard about him throughout the years.

He knew he wasn't a saint, but he was a very good attorney. He was as brilliant as he was dangerous. The mere mention of Geno's name sent chills throughout the Judge's physical being.

When he hired Geno to represent his son in his rape case, the Judge knew he made a deal with the devil, but at the time he had no other choice. His son was in a bind and he needed someone with the right amount of power and influence to get him out of his legal mess. Geno told him upfront when he took on his son's case that he would owe him a favor if he got his son a more than favorable plea deal. Geno delivered as promised. True to his word, he sent Solomon to cash in his marker with the Judge because his back was against the wall. Judge Bukowski had a choice to make. If he refused to grant Geno's request, the consequences could prove to be fatal. His choice was not really a choice. It was an inevitable reality and something he had to do if he wanted to continue to live his peaceful life and not incur Geno's wrath.

"What is it that he needs from me?" he asked.

The two men walked over to a quiet corner of the room to continue their conversation. Solomon relayed Geno's request to him verbatim. Judge Bukowski absorbed every word, playing close attention to every detail. The Judge grimaced at the request, because it required him to do something against his better judgment and would weigh heavily on his spirit. Before he responded to Solomon, he glanced around to make sure no one could hear their conversation. Once he was sure the coast was clear, Judge Bukowski decided to respond.

"Young man, you can tell our mutual friend I'll do what he asks. I want you to also make it clear to him that once I do this he and I are squared away," Judge Bukowski whispered loud enough for only Solomon to hear. With men like Geno, no debt was ever paid in full. Every favor granted was merely a down payment for another bill to be due at a later date.

"I will relay that message to him. I appreciate you taking out the time to speak to me. I hope you enjoy the rest of your evening," Solomon stated before he shook the Judge's hand and walked away.

He felt relieved when he heard the Judge's affirmative response to Geno's request. Once he had a chance to talk to Geno, he knew he would be pleased with him and what he was able to accomplish on his behalf. After he relieved himself in the restroom, he walked back over to the table where Jia was seated. Even while behind bars, Geno just gave him a lesson on how to get things done that he never learned in law school. This knowledge would serve him well in his future law career. For now, he just wanted to enjoy the rest of the evening with his beautiful companion, Jia.

Chapter 11

Sal looked very relaxed seated in Geno's chair with his feet up on his desk. He had become quite comfortable with his newfound authority as the head man in charge of the Caprese Foundation while Geno's future hung in the balance. A part of him wondered how it would feel to have that position permanently. The title of CEO with his name attached seemed to fit him well. Just the thought of being in control of a business entity that generated hundreds of millions of dollars in revenue per year could be almost as intoxicating and seductive as a drug to any man.

Sal had no clue how Geno's legal situation would play out, but he hoped for the best for him for the most part. There was still a selfish, power hungry side to him that yearned for the spotlight and adulation Geno received being such an influential man. He wanted to be more than just Geno's second in charge. He had a bigger vision of how he hoped his future would play out. He didn't see his quest to be a boss on Geno's level as a sense of betrayal to Geno in the same manner that Silvio and Pappi did when they hatched their scheme to unseat Geno from the throne. Unlike them, he was there with Geno every step of the way on his rise to the top. He put in work to earn his position.

In all honesty, Sal did help Geno build the Foundation into what it had become and felt entitled to a larger share of the pie or at least to have a pie of his own. He saw his ascent to the top of the food chain as a natural progression he had a right to pursue. After all, Geno had many years to be the big man and now Sal felt it was his time to shine. It was just unfortunate his thirst for power occurred when Geno was at what appeared to be his weakest position ever being that he was currently incarcerated. Geno always taught him that the wisest businessmen always took advantage of their rival's shortcoming or mishaps. Sal reasoned he was just following the wise guidance he was given by his mentor. Never would Geno imagine his own words would be used against him by his own comrade.

Unbeknownst to Geno, Sal already had a few irons in the pan of his own outside of the Caprese Foundation that showed great potential. He took some of the money he earned from the Foundation and hired an outside business attorney in Los Angeles to set up a dummy corporation which would serve as a front for the business venture he planned to launch in the near future. He modeled his company after the Caprese Foundation with its structure and diversified business portfolio. In fact, one of the business ventures he planned to shell a good amount of money into was a video gaming company to compete with CITD in the gaming industry. He planned to start the company from the grown up using hungry college students eager to get their gaming ideas into the free market. Sal knew this wouldn't sit well with Geno no matter how he tried to explain it to him. Geno hated competition, especially from someone who knew many of his business secrets.

Sal would definitely have a bounty on his head if Geno found out about his new company and how Sal used money from the Foundation as start-up capital. That was why Sal chose to keep his plan under wraps until the right time. Geno getting arrested was sort of a stroke of good luck for him because he could be free to get his business off the ground without Geno having a chance to find out or to attempt to stop his momentum. Sal knew it was wrong to partially hope for Geno's downfall, but he also had his own aspirations for greatness. The time was ripe for him to act. He just needed to be meticulous and shrewd with every step he took.

He learned at the foot of a master. Now it was his chance to make manifest the fruits of his many lessons.

Sal busied himself web surfing on Geno's computer until he was interrupted by the door to Geno's office opening up. It was Jia. She dropped the stack of papers in her hands when she saw him behind Geno's desk. She was startled to see Sal in Geno's office. No one was normally allowed in there but her when Geno wasn't around. She bent down on the floor to pick up the pile of papers she had dropped. Sal eyes lit up at the sight of her butt raised up in the air. Her dress also rose up slightly to reveal her shapely thighs. He took his hand and rubbed his crotch and licked his lips. Sal wanted to get a taste of Jia's sweetness for quite some time. However, she rebuffed every one of his advances.

"I'm sorry, Sal, I had no clue you were in here. Mr. Caprese usually keeps his office closed. I just came in to get a few papers that needed to be filed away," Jia stated, obviously shaken up. Sal always made her nervous because the way he looked her was creepy to say the least. She just saw him as a dirty old man. The thought of having sex with him made her want to puke.

"It's alright, pretty young thing. While Geno is out of commission, I'm in charge of things around here. Everything that you do for him, you can do for me," he stated suggestively.

Sal got up from behind the desk and walked over to where Jia was. He kneeled down on the floor to help her out. He stood up at the same time she did. He took his arm and wrapped it around her waist. His hand slid down a little lower so he could grab her derriere. Jia's entire body tensed up. She couldn't believe he could be so bold.

"Mr. Sal, what are you doing? That is highly inappropriate. Please let me go!" she demanded. She tried to pull away, but Sal pulled her closer to him.

"When are you going to stop teasing me, baby? You know I want you. I just want to get some of that sweet little kitten down there. Don't fight it, baby. Just let me get a taste," he begged. His lust for Jia had consumed him over the years and brought him to finally act out on it in such a reckless manner. Somehow, Jia managed to summon up the strength to free herself from his grasp. She took a step back to catch her breath. She felt violated by Sal's actions. He had flirted with her on numerous occasions, but this time he had crossed the line.

"Sal, you need to stop. Don't ever touch me like that again. It is never going to happen between me and you. I don't look at you in a sexual manner at all. I never have and I never will. Besides, I have a boyfriend. Please respect my relationship," Jia stated firmly as she fixed her clothing. She was upset because she didn't deserve to be treated like a cheap sex object. She was a highly intelligent young woman and always conducted herself in a professional manner at work. Sal was totally out of line.

"Who are you talking about, Solomon? He's just a little boy. You need a real man in your life to make you scream and holler," he asserted. Jia was not amused.

"This is the last straw, Sal. I have tried to ignore your sexual advances toward me, but enough is enough. When Mr. Caprese comes back, I plan to tell him about your behavior," she threatened. Sal facial expression turned from one of laughter to a look of pure evil in an instant.

"Geno is jail and won't be back in this office anytime soon, if at all. I'm in charge while he's gone. Besides, if you breathe one word of this to him you little bitch, you and that little boyfriend of yours will come up missing. Now get the hell out of here!" Sal stated angrily.

The tone of his voice and his body language let her know he was for real. She knew what kind of men he and Geno were. She knew he would make good on his threat if she did tell Geno. Jia was scared to death and didn't know what to do. Even though Geno was a gangster, he always treated her with the utmost of respect. Sal, on the other hand, was a typical street thug who believed in bullying people to get what he wanted.

Jia hoped Sal would catch a stray bullet between his eyes one day. It would be his just due for being such a pervert. She raced out of the office in a hurry and almost ran into Cesare and Jericho. They were on their way to have a meeting with Sal. She had no clue they caught the tail end of what just transpired. She glanced in Cesare's direction as she made her way back to her office. She didn't have to say a word. Her facial expression and the tears streaming down her cheeks said more than enough.

"What the hell was that about, Sal?" Cesare asked. He sensed something wasn't right.

"I just told her something she didn't want to hear is all. You know how females get so emotional over everything. However, that's nothing for you to be concerned about. You need to mind your own business. You two have your own problems with me I want to address. Come on in here," he replied in a snippy tone. Cesare was a little dazed by Sal's brazen demeanor. He wasn't acting like the calm, composed Sal who played the role of his mentor when he first came to work at the Foundation. This was a totally different person standing in front of him right now.

Cesare followed behind Sal into Geno's office with Jericho pulling up the rear. Jericho couldn't stand the sight of Sal, but maintained his calm at all times around him. Sal had disrespected him one too many times for no justifiable reason. That was a death sentence for any man that crossed Jericho's path. In his mind, he had already mapped out a plan of how he wanted to kill him if given the green light by Geno to do so. Even though he and Geno had developed a good relationship thus far, he and Sal had a much longer history of friendship together. They were in the trenches together for years in the heat of many street wars. It would take a lot more than a few disrespectful words from Sal toward him for Geno to give Jericho permission to kill him. For now, Jericho chose to remain silent and take Sal's snubs on the chin. He was a patient man. His best work over the years took place when he let his victims marinate and stew for awhile before he made his move.

Jericho's gut instinct told him something wasn't right with Sal, but he didn't say a thing to Cesare. He had the gift of being able to read a man's eyes to see his intentions. When he looked at Sal, he saw a hunger for power consuming his soul. However, he wanted to see how Sal played his hand first to prove his suspicions were right before he said anything to Geno or Cesare. His suspicions were confirmed when he noticed how Sal chose to meet with them in Geno's office and not his own. Sal's behavior sent a clear message he had designs on

Geno's seat as the King and planned to come for the top seat. Jericho had no intention of allowing that to happen. Since they met, Geno was a solid, stand up guy who was true to his word with everything he promised him. He was also now a member of his family and Jericho always guarded his loved ones with his own life. He took a seat next to Cesare across from Sal. He was intrigued to hear what this impromptu meeting was all about.

"So, what's up, Sal? What is this meeting about? Is there a problem with security that I need to be aware of?" Jericho inquired. He could tell his presence made Sal nervous.

"This meeting is not about any security issues. I did, however, get a call from John Lucci this morning that has me pissed the hell off. He told me about his meeting with you two and how you wanted him to try and locate Sam Bradford. Whose brilliant idea was that?" Sal inquired.

"It was my idea, Sal. That rat needs to die. He's the reason Geno is behind bars. If we get rid of him, the Feds have no case. What's your issue with what we did?" Cesare replied.

"So, you're a killer now, huh? The problem, Cesare, is you don't take it upon yourself to make those kinds of move on behalf of this organization. There's a reason there's a thing called a chain of command in place. You don't make those types of decisions without consulting with me first. Since

Geno's not here, let me be clear so I don't have to repeat this again, I am in charge," Sal replied.

His authoritative tone surprised Cesare. He sounded like a man drunk with power. He never saw this side to Sal before. Regardless of what Sal said or how he felt about Cesare's actions, Geno was his brother. He didn't regret his decision to reach out to John Lucci. He would do whatever was necessary to get Geno out of jail. He had never killed a man before, but he would do so if it meant saving his brother's life. He glanced over at Jericho. He wasn't moved by Sal's rant. He just sat there with an emotionless look on face.

"I don't see what the problem is, Sal. Don't you want Geno back on the streets?" Cesare asked.

"I was thinking the same thing, Cesare," Jericho chimed in before Sal could respond. He wanted to add more fuel to the fire to see how Sal responded. Jericho played close attention to Sal's body language and the tone of his speech. Every subtle detail revealed something about Sal he planned to use against him one day if necessary.

"Of course I want to see Geno free. What kind of asinine question is that to ask me? What you don't understand is that Sam is under federal protection and if we make a move on him while the Feds have him and we fail, all hell will break loose. Not only will Geno be up shit's creek, but so will the rest of us. The Feds were just up in here going through our files and computers. We don't need them coming back again," Sal reasoned.

"That's what I'm here for, Sal. I can get the job done in a way nobody will know a thing. My work speaks for itself," Jericho stated confidently. Sal dismissed his statement and continued to speak as though Jericho wasn't even in the room.

"When and if we make a move like this, it has to be done with the utmost precision so no mistakes are made. You know nothing about these kinds of things, Cesare. You've never been in the trenches of battle in your life. Stick to what you know best and that's playing video games with Jeremy. If we make a move on Sam, it will be my call. Are we clear, Jericho?" Sal asked.

"We're crystal clear, Boss. Is that all?" Jericho replied for both him and Cesare.

"That's all for now. Let me be. I have work to do," he replied.

Jericho and Cesare got up to exit Geno's office after the tongue lashing they just received from Sal. They paid his threat no mind. They had every intention of killing Sam Bradford with or without Sal's permission. The problem was, thus far, John Lucci was unable to locate him. He had reached out to all of his resources in law enforcement with no success. The Feds had Sam stowed away at a very remote location somewhere that was off the radar. However, Jericho had an ace up his sleeve. He planned to make a few moves on his own utilizing his own contacts to try and get a location for Sam. They didn't give a damn about what Sal said. Jericho didn't need his blessing for this kind of mission. This was his area of expertise. Geno would be a free man soon if they had their way. Once Geno was home, then the three of them could decide what to do about Sal.

Chapter 12

Geno was back in court in front of Judge Artest once again. Solomon was successful in getting him to agree to a second bail hearing. He hoped the outcome would be different from their last encounter because he was out of his comfort zone being locked in a jail cell. He couldn't think clearly surrounded by a world filled with madness. The food tasted like garbage compared to the fancy meals he was used to eating. His back ached from sleeping on the thin, stiff mattress on his bunk as opposed to the California king-sized gel foam mattress he rested on at his estate. While he enjoyed his entertaining conversations with his young cellmate, Remy, it was time for him to be out on the streets where he was most effective and at his best. He was extremely optimistic about his chances of being released on bail today.

Geno listened carefully as Mayhem wrapped up his arguments as to why he should be denied bail once again. He stuck with the same script as before when he contended that Geno was a flight risk and a menace to society even though he knew Geno had no intention of fleeing the country. Anybody who knew Geno Caprese knew that wasn't in his character. Geno was the kind of man who would stand and face his charges before the court like a man and fight tooth and nail for his freedom. Nonetheless, Mayhem sought to have any advantage he could over Geno if he hoped to win this case. With Geno behind bars, he reasoned, he wouldn't have access to all of the many resources he would have at his disposal to mount as strong of a defense for himself if he were on the streets. Satisfied with his arguments before the Judge, Mayhem returned to his seat.

Once Mayhem was done stating the federal government's position on Geno's request for bail, it was Solomon's chance to present his case. Geno observed his every action and utterance as he argued on his behalf. Geno beamed with pride at his young bull at the way he took charge of the courtroom like an attorney seasoned well beyond the few years he had been in practice. He was genuinely impressed. In addition to presenting compelling arguments on Geno's behalf, Solomon was also successful in getting several of Geno's business partners to attest to his upstanding character. He got a few well respected community leaders who could vouch for all of the charity work Geno and the Foundation did across Baltimore City. Once they all completed their testimony on Geno's behalf, Solomon sat down next to him.

"How did I do?" Solomon asked nervously.

"You did well, Solomon. I don't think we have a thing to worry about at all. When I get out of here, you and I are going out for a big steak dinner. For now, just relax and let's see how this all plays out," Geno replied confidently. The Judge's decision could go either way, but he didn't appear to be worried at all. They all stood up as Judge Artest readied himself to speak. He had made his decision and was prepared to address the court.

"Now that I have heard arguments from both sides about this matter, I have made up my mind. It is the Court's position that Mr. Caprese is not a flight risk as he has documented that he has very strong ties to the community. After carefully reconsideration of this matter, I am setting his bail at three million dollars. Once bail has been posted, Mr. Caprese will be released under the terms and conditions set forth by the Court until his trial date has been set. That is my decision and so shall it stand."

"Your Honor, you are making a mistake. I ask that you please reconsider. This man is a sociopath. He is a pariah and a genuine menace to the community. If you put him back on the streets, the life of my main witness in this case will be in jeopardy. Please don't do this, Judge. I strongly urge you to reconsider. It is in the best interest of the community that he remains in custody. This is an issue of public safety," Mayhem argued in a last ditch effort.

He was not pleased at all with the Judge's decision. In fact, he was rather surprised the Judge chose to grant Geno bail given the arrangement they had already agreed to prior to his first hearing. Mayhem paid Judge Artest twenty-five thousand dollars in cash to ensure Geno would not see the streets again before his trial date. He had never bribed a Judge before, but he was desperate to convict Geno by any means necessary. To see Judge Artest welch on their deal got him heated, but there was nothing he could do. He faced losing his law license if his actions were uncovered. Not only was Geno a free man, but he was out twenty-five grand with nothing to show for his efforts.

"Mr. Mayhem, I hear your concerns, but you have not presented any hard evidence to suggest that your witness' life is in danger or shown how Mr. Caprese is a threat to the community. However, Mr. Caprese has had a host of well respected individuals speak on his behalf to testify to his character and his willingness to stand trial and face the allegations levied against him. You have had ample time to convince me otherwise, but you have not provided me with any documentation. That is just the facts. My decision is final in this matter," the Judge stated to reaffirm his position.

His words clearly did not match his facial expression. He knew everything Mayhem said about Geno being a thug was true, but there was nothing he could do. He was disappointed he had to allow Geno to make bail, but he had no choice in the matter. The damning information his longtime friend and fellow judge, Lance Bukowski, had on him forced him to grant Geno bail regardless of his desire to do just the opposite. Judge Bukowski met with him recently and threatened to reveal how he covertly rented out several of his investment properties in the City to a Russian sex trafficking ring and how he used his power and influence as a Judge to help them avoid prosecution if he didn't set Geno free. If this information hit the press, it would destroy his legacy and possibly send him to jail.

At first he was shocked his old friend would use this damning information against him to go to bat for a scum bag like Geno, but when Judge Bukowski explained his debt to Geno, he understood. It was the price one had to pay when he made a deal with a man like Geno Caprese. Besides, he reasoned that Judge Bukowski would now owe him a favor in return. He had every intention of collecting on it one day. This was just business as usual in the world of society's power brokers. These types of behind the scenes deals took place more often than the average person could imagine. How cases were decided was not decided by actual innocence or guilt, but by which side of the law wielded the most power and influence in a given situation.

"Your Honor, I appreciate your fairness in this matter. I give you my word you have not made a mistake allowing me to make bail until I can have my day in court to prove my innocence," Geno stated with a smirk on his face.

"I sure hope so, Mr. Caprese. It would certainly be in your best interest to not jump bail because if you fail to comply with any the stipulations set forth for your release, I will not hesitate to revoke your bail and issue a warrant for your arrest," Judge Artest promised him. That was a promise he would make good on if Geno gave him ample reason to do so.

"I will personally make sure my client fully complies with all of the terms set for his release, Sir," Solomon butted in.

As the Judge dismissed the court session, Geno couldn't hide his feelings of excitement at the fact he would be going home shortly. He had worked his magic once again. He was glad to be free to go home and spend time with Carina and his two children. He also needed to get back to the office to resume control of the daily operations of the Foundation. He yearned to walk out of the front door of the courthouse to taste a breath of fresh air as opposed to the stale stench of his jail cell which he had to endure for the past month.

The past thirty something days seemed like thirty years to a man who was used to coming and going as he pleased. If he had his way, he had no intention of seeing the inside of jail cell ever again in his life. This was truly a humbling experience for him he would never forget. He counted down the minutes for Solomon to do what was necessary for his bail to be paid so he could be released from this hell hole. This was just a small victory for him because he still had to stand trial, but it was a step in the right direction.

Once he hit the streets, he planned to work a few more miracles to beat the case the government had against him. Sitting in a cell gave him a lot of time to think and strategize. He was ready to do battle with Mayhem. Judge Artest honestly wanted to flash Geno the middle finger in front of the entire audience in the courtroom for using his good friend Lance against him, but opted against doing so. Every dog had his day and he couldn't wait for Geno to get his just due. However, he would have to wait for another day because the Angels of mercy showed Geno favor today. Judge Artest looked at Geno with a mean scowl as he was escorted out of his courtroom.

Chapter 13

Geno felt like he was on top of the world at the moment. One could compare the jubilation he felt to the happiness that ran through Floyd Mayweather after he cashed his nine figure check after defeating Manny Pacquiao in the boxing match of the century. When he stepped out of the courthouse, he was flanked by Solomon, Cesare, Sal, and a team of new bodyguards that were recently hired and trained by Jericho. He was greeted by a mob of eager members of the press and a crowd of over two hundred of his ardent supporters. They anxiously awaited a statement of some sort from him. He had been silent thus far throughout this entire ordeal, but now that he was free, he felt it was time for him to address the media.

The people had heard all over the news all of the negative allegations that Mayhem levied against him and now it was his turn to give them his side of the story. If he wanted to swing public opinion in his favor and paint the picture of himself as being the victim of a witch hunt by the federal government, then this was his time to do so. He lived for moments like this. Seizing the opportunity to address the crowd, Geno took a brief spell to collect his thoughts before he spoke. After he composed himself, he decided it was time for him to speak. His words weren't rehearsed or prewritten. They came straight from the gut.

"I know you all have heard a lot about me in the press in the past few weeks and all of it has painted me as a tax dodging thug who runs a criminal organization. I just want to say that none of what you have heard about me is true. I pay my taxes every year and I have never been involved in any form of organized criminal activity or been a part of any crime family. However, I am a man who believes in the concept of family because that is my foundation. My beautiful wife, Carina, is my rock I have leaned on for support throughout this witch hunt. My children, Gianna and Stefan, kept me motivated every day I sat in that cell unjustly waiting to make bail. This attack on my character and financial affairs that has been launched against me by federal prosecutor, Gavin Mayhem, because of a personal vendetta he has against me for something I can admit to today that I was guilty of doing in my past life. You see, when I was a younger man, I was in a relationship with his

daughter, Amy. We were two young college students with big ambitions who fell head over heels in love. We had talked about getting married, but those plans changed when I met an amazing woman who would one day become my wife. When I first met my wonderful wife, Carina, I was captivated by her smile. Regretfully, I can admit today before you all that I broke Amy's heart by being unfaithful to her with Carina. I betrayed her love for me and, as a result, she endured a host of emotional and psychological issues due to my actions. I am ashamed of what I did to have caused her so much grief due to my selfish actions. I have apologized to her and my wife in the past in private, but today I want to publicly apologize to both of them and ask for forgiveness. I also want to apologize to Mr. Mayhem publicly as well for the pain he felt as a father. We all fall short at times in life, but should a man be made to suffer like federal prosecutor Mayhem is attempting to make me do today for a mistake made in the past? I am guilty of breaking his daughter's heart but I am not guilty of the trumped up charges he has made against me which call into question my integrity and respectable reputation as an attorney and businessman in the Baltimore community. Prosecutor Mayhem has even went so far as to get a trusted business associate of mine to turn against me. This business associate, who shall remain nameless, got caught breaking the law and has worked with the federal government to try and frame me in exchange for a lighter sentence for himself. This case is based on the word of an admitted criminal. I know that the federal government has been after me for years because I'm young, rich, and successful and I'm not afraid to challenge them, along with the Baltimore City police department, in court. I have taken them both to task for their brutality and manufactured drug cases that they've tried to pin on a host of my clients and beat them every time using the same legal system they claim to represent. Check my record and you will see I am speaking the truth. For as much wealth as I have been blessed to acquire for myself and my family, I have been just as generous in giving back to the city of Baltimore mightily to countless social organizations and human service providers dedicated to the betterment of our City. Please don't rush to judgment before all of the facts come out. I am not a monster. I have been a consistent advocate in the legal system for the poor and downtrodden. Thank you for allowing me a chance to address you today. I look forward to my day in court to clear my name."

The crowd erupted in applause as Geno made his exit. He decided not to field any questions. His security detail cleared a pathway for him to walk down the steps to his limousine. Clay got out from the driver's side of the vehicle to open the door for him to hop inside. His entourage followed suit and joined him inside of the limo. His bodyguards hopped in a second vehicle to follow closely behind them. Geno sat back and rested his head on the soft leather headrest as he reflected on his speech with pride.

Judging by the reaction of the crowd to his words, Geno's message resonated loudly to the people that he was a victim of a character assassination attempt by the federal government and a reckless federal prosecutor with an axe to grind. With the number of racially motivated police killings of Black men and cases of police misconduct that were reported on the news lately against average citizens regardless of race, his assertion didn't seem too far-fetched. The average Baltimorean who lived in the inner city already had deeply rooted distrust of law enforcement officers and the legal system in general. One thing Geno had in his favor was his long standing ties to the community. He was respected in the Black community for his philanthropic efforts as much as he was in the White community. He believed in sharing his wealth with the masses. He was a man of the people and for the people. He had the community behind him. If necessary, he planned to work with local community leaders who were in his hip pocket to stage protests in front of the courthouse every day of his trial in an effort to shift the focus from himself and his alleged crimes to Mayhem and his personal vendetta against him. He had no problem playing the victim if it meant he would be exonerated in a court of law.

"Damn, I'm glad to be out of that place. Solomon you did well, young man. You are a star on the rise," Geno stated happily. He looked forward to having a chance to further groom him for greatness.

"Thanks, Geno, but I couldn't have made it happen without your help," Solomon admitted honestly. He knew it was Geno's bringing Judge Bukowski into the mix that made his freedom a reality.

"That's true, but you held your own going word for word with a vet like Mayhem, who is probably somewhere crying his eyes out right now. So, how was my speech?" Geno asked.

"You had them eating out of the palm of your hands, Geno!" Cesare interjected into the mix.

"What can I say, Geno, you did what you do best. You took away some of Mayhem's momentum going into this trial and made him your bitch for the world to see. He is going to be pissed," Sal joked.

"Fuck Mayhem and the United States government. When I'm done with this case, I'm gonna make Mayhem wish he had retired years ago and left me the hell alone. I'm gonna have his law license once this is all over. I might even sue the government and make them empty out the Federal Reserve for me. I still can't believe Sam is a goddamn rat. That ungrateful bastard snitched on me after all of the money he made working for us. I'll be damned if I let him destroy what I worked so hard to build," Geno ranted on.

Sal wasn't happy with Geno's last comment. He was offended Geno only gave himself credit for building the Caprese Foundation into the powerful organization it had become. While it was true Geno was the driving force, he felt he played just as significant role in the overall success of the Foundation. His statement drove home to him even more it was time for him to strike out on his own if he wanted to get the level of respect he felt he deserved.

"Speaking on that subject, Geno, I think you need to have a talk with your brother here. It seems as though him and the other one, Jericho, got it in their minds they were going to take out Sam on their own without your permission. I tried to explain to them how that was a bad idea and how it would draw even more heat on us from the Feds. Besides, could you see Cesare here actually catching a body? Anyhow, I squashed their plan before they were able to act on it to save us another headache to have to deal with on top of your trial," Sal boasted in hopes Geno would cosign his actions. Cesare didn't say a word. The menacing look on his face displayed his animosity toward Sal for attempting to embarrass him and Jericho in front of Geno.

"Sal, actually that wasn't a bad idea. The young bulls had it right. That motherfucker needs to get got. He's the reason I'm in this mess. As for my brother, Cesare, yeah it's true that he's not a killer by nature, but he's a Caprese by blood. We will kill anything that threatens our family if the situation presents itself. You better never let me hear you question the heart of my little brother again. Besides, when did you become afraid to mix it up with the Feds?" Geno inquired. Cesare nodded his head in agreement with Geno. He was glad to see Geno take up for him as well.

"I'm not afraid of a thing, Geno. I think you know this already. I was just being cautious and thinking before we act like you always say we should do. I think it's way too dangerous to try something like that right now with so much heat on us already. That's just my opinion, but you're the Boss," Sal responded. He and Geno were usually on the same page with these matters, but clearly something had changed. Being in jail and having to ponder the possibility of serving a prison sentence had a way of impacting one's perception of reality and the sense of urgency to act to avoid such a fate.

"I respect your opinion, but I have the final word on this matter. Sam has to go. I can't afford to have him running his mouth in front of a jury. I want him done now," Geno stated emphatically.

"There's a slight problem, Geno. We don't know where the Feds are holding Sam. Lucci came up empty with his people when your brothers put him on the case," Sal stated.

"That's not a problem at all, Sal. While I was in the joint, a little birdie gave me some information as to where the Feds are hiding him. Once he is out of the picture, this whole case goes away. All of the evidence they have is just circumstantial without him around to connect the dots. We need to move fast because now that I'm free, I'm sure Mayhem will be relocating him soon so we can't get to him. Sal, I want you to fall back on this one. I want Jericho and Cesare to run point on this. It's time for our little brother to get his feet wet," Geno uttered.

"I'm ready for the job, Geno. Say no more. I will link up with Jericho and get it done," Cesare stated without a trace of fear in his voice. He had a point to prove with Sal testing his mettle in front of Geno. For the rest of the ride, they filled Geno in on current events at the office. Sal was insulted Geno told him to stand down for this mission. It became clear to Sal his role would begin to decrease in the organization because Geno had his own vision of how the leadership of the Foundation would look in the future and it didn't appear to include him. Their conversation further reinforced to him it was time for him to make his own moves.

Chapter 14

After he had Clay drop Cesare, Sal, and Solomon off at their destinations, Geno headed home to be with his wife, Carina. She eagerly awaited his arrival. He was so physically exhausted, he fell asleep in the back of the limo while Clay made his way to his estate. His forty minute power nap served his body well. When he reached the gated entrance to Geno's residence, Clay rolled down the privacy divider because he decided it was time to wake him up out of his slumber.

"Geno, we've arrived at your palace, Boss!" he yelled loudly. The sound of his voice startled Geno. He opened his eyes and glanced around to survey his property.

"Man, it feels good to be home!" he exclaimed loudly. He fully extended out his arms and legs to loosen up his limbs and let out a loud yawn.

"I'm glad you're home as well, Geno. I was kinda bored not being able to chauffeur you around town," Clay said jokingly. He drove the limo up the long driveway and parked it in front of his mansion. Clay hoped he could own a home half as nice as the Caprese estate one day.

"Well, if I get my way, you will be very busy from here on out because I have no intention of going back to that God forsaken place called prison. Go get yourself something to eat and take a few hours to relax, Clay. I'll be tied up here for awhile with the wife. I'll give you a call when I need you."

"Okay, Boss."

Geno opened the car door himself and got out of the limo. He waved to Clay as he pulled off and drove back down the driveway. He slowly walked toward the front door and rung the bell. It took all of two minutes before the most beautiful woman in the world appeared before his eyes. Carina Caprese looked like a goddess who was uniquely crafted for him by the Big Man in the sky above.

"Hey there, beautiful," he stated as he almost tripped over his own feet when he tried to reach his arms out to hug her.

"Get your handsome self in here now. Baby, I have missed you so freaking much," Carina uttered.

She was overcome with a mix of emotions. She smiled, cried, and screamed out loud all in a matter of seconds. She looked upward and thanked God for answering her prayers to bring her Geno home to her. She jumped into his arms and kissed all over him. Geno was overwhelmed by her affection, but enjoyed every minute of it all. Neither one of them wanted this moment to end.

"I see somebody missed me."

"Yes, I did miss you. Let me show you how much."

Carina wasn't in the mood for a lot of small talk. The children were still in school and they had the house to themselves to do as they pleased. She slowly began to undress right in the foyer of their home. First, she unbuttoned her top and tossed it to the side. Next, she untied her sweatpants and let them drop to the floor. She stood before Geno in her bra and panties as a majestic sight to behold. Geno's heart began to race with lustful anticipation of what he planned to do to her. His penis began to bulge inside of his pants. He didn't need any foreplay to get aroused. Just the sight of Carina's curvy figure was enough for him.

Geno took Carina by the hand and guided her to the staircase. He sat down on the fourth step from the bottom and instructed her to sit on his lap while he playfully fondled her breasts through her bra. He planted passionate kisses all up and down her neck, her chest, and the region right above her crotch. Carina held onto his muscular shoulders and leaned backward so he could tease her panty line with his tongue. Geno ripped off her bra and roughly took her breasts into his mouth. Carina's hard nipples were delighted by the sensations evoked when his tongue pressed against them. The moisture between her thighs began to flow freely as his firm hands fondled her body gently.

"Take me, baby. I want you to taste me. Lick me until I cream all over your face."

Geno loved when she talked raunchily to him. He got up from his seated position and sat her down on the steps. He slowly pulled down her panties and spread her legs apart. He took a moment to admire her neatly shaven vagina. It had been over a month since he laid eyes on Carina's treasure chest. His mouth watered for a taste of her juices. When his tongue touched her clit, Carina's body became so limp she almost slid down the steps. Geno cupped his hands under her bottom to stop her from sliding and proceeded to bury his head in between her thighs. Every lick from his tongue hit just the right spot. He took Carina down a road to ecstasy that she desperately needed to experience. She came over and over and again and again. After going over a month with no sex and being surrounded by nothing but men, Geno was hornier than he had ever been in his entire life. He almost came on himself just from hearing Carina say his name in a sultry tone while he pleasured her with his mouth.

"You are something else, Mrs. Caprese. Damn, you taste good!" he stated when he stopped performing cunnilingus on her for a moment to catch his breath.

Geno's member was harder than a boulder. Carina turned around and got down on her knees so he could enter her doggy style. Geno's stiffness slid right into her wetness with no problem at all. Her kitten was ready for him to service her like only he could. Every time he thrust himself inside of her, Geno released a smidgen of the frustration he felt the entire time he was locked up.

He flipped Carina over like a ragdoll and entered her once again. Geno delivered shockwaves of erotic bliss throughout Carina's body for almost thirty minutes before he felt like he was almost ready to cum. Just as he was about to release his semen inside of her, he bent down to bite her nipples again. Carina shed tears of joy and pulled him in closer to her. She rocked her hips in sync with his strokes. Even though she had already had at least five orgasms already, she felt another rush of uncontrollable emotions filtered throughout her loins. They both climaxed together.

"What the hell are you doing?" Geno asked as he saw Carina get up and position herself in front of him. She took his manhood into her mouth and proceeded to swallow every drop of his love fluids that he didn't release inside of her. It was her way of reminding him just how much he meant to her. She sucked on his manhood until he was erect again.

"I'm here to service my man like he needs to be serviced. Geno Caprese, promise me you will never make me miss you like this again," she pleaded.

"I promise you, baby. I promise you I will never leave you alone like this again. My word is my bond."

Geno ran his fingers through her hair and gently caressed her face. He knew Carina worried herself sick about him the entire time he was in jail. He wished she didn't have to go through this rough ordeal with him because she didn't deserve to suffer in the least bit. She was his empress who shared the helm of the Caprese Empire and stood right by his side as his equal in all ways. He planted tender kisses on her lips as his way of apologizing for her heartache and sorrow. Carina closed her eyes and held onto him like it was the last time she would ever see him again. She was ready for another round of mind blowing sex. She mounted his penis and it disappeared inside of her. Geno wrapped his hands around her waist and proceeded to grind inside of her. He got up from the steps and began to walk down the stairs toward the fireplace so he could have his way with her some more. They had the rest of the day to sex each other into a coma.

Chapter 15

Jericho normally liked to work alone when he stalked his victims and carried out an execution. However, he brought Cesare along with him for his current assignment. This was his way of testing him out before they had to take out Sam Bradford. Since Geno wanted Cesare in on the job, Jericho had to make sure he was up for the task. There was no better way for him to test him out than to see him in action. He glanced over at Cesare and could sense the fear that consumed his heart and entire being.

Cesare tried his best to not let his nervousness show, but it was obvious. His legs shook uncontrollably. The palms of his hands were sweaty. He wished he could smoke a cigarette to calm himself down, but Jericho didn't allow anyone to smoke in his truck. Jericho could relate to what he experienced. He went through the same thing right before he killed his first target. The first time he took a life seemed like a lifetime ago for Jericho because he was now a master of the art of causing death. He no longer felt fear or any sense of remorse for his victims, but was, in fact, excited about getting to that very moment when his victims took their last breath. He personified the very essence of what a psychiatrist would describe as a psychopath.

"Don't be nervous, bro, I've got you. All you have to do is follow my lead," Jericho said as his way of easing Cesare's mind.

"Is it that obvious that I'm nervous?" Cesare asked.

"You are shaking like a leaf. It's natural to feel that way. You've never done this before. Trust me, once we set this thing in motion, those nerves will disappear. You won't have time to feel a thing. All you will be focused on is getting the job done," Jericho promised him.

"Jericho, you are crazy as hell, man. How can you be so calm and okay with killing people?" Cesare inquired.

"Because, little bro, this is what I do and I've been paid a ton of money for how well I handle my business. I'ma virtuoso at this thing here, brother. One day I'll explain it all to you, how I got to be this way, but right now it's time to go to work. Are you sure you wanna do this?" Jericho asked for confirmation. Once he got started on an assignment, there was no turning back.

"Yeah, I'm good," Cesare replied.

"Let's get to it then. There's our target right there," Jericho replied and pointed in the direction of a tall, dark skinned Black man walking away from the football field headed toward his vehicle. The man had just finished playing a game of flag football and said his goodbyes to the others players. When Cesare glanced a little closer at the man they were about to kill, he recognized his face and got even more nervous. As soon as the man pulled off, Jericho slowly followed behind him in a cautious manner so as to not draw attention to himself.

"Yo, Jericho, I know that guy. That dude is a cop. His name is Swift or something. He's the one who arrested me when they tried to pin my old girlfriend's murder on me. You seriously plan to kill a cop? If we get caught, they will fry our asses!"

"Be easy, Cesare. I've got this. I never get caught. I'm a professional at this thing here. Just like Geno is the man in that courtroom, I'm the man in this murder game. That's why they call me the Smooth Assassin. I get in and out like a phantom. I'm just a figment of my victim's imagination. They never see me coming."

Ever since the day Detective Swift pulled him over, Jericho noticed him tailing him on several other occasions. He never let on to him that he saw him following him. Swift was unrelenting in his pursuit of answers in the Harrison case. Jericho surmised that he was more than likely working the case off the books considering the fact Geno's mark was already serving time for the crime. The last thing he needed was for Swift to be on his tail when he went after Sam Bradford. Consequently, he had to be eliminated.

To best prepare himself for the job, Jericho decided to do his own counterintelligence surveillance of Swift. He hired Gutta to tail Swift to track his comings and goings on a daily basis and to break into his apartment to see if there were any intimate details of his private life they could use against him. Swift never picked up the fact he was being following. Gutta discovered every Thursday after work Swift followed the same routine. He played a game of flag football with a group of friends on the football field at the high school located a few blocks away from where he lived. Afterwards, he would stop and get a six pack of beer to drink. Then he headed home to watch ESPN before he fell fast asleep on his living room couch with his remote control in his hand. He always left his gun holstered on a coat rack near the front door. Since he lived on the first floor of a two story house, it was easy for Gutta to spy on him through the living room window. Gutta also observed that the apartment on the upper level was vacant, which meant there would be no witnesses close by if they decided to kill him there.

Like clockwork, Swift followed the same routine today. As soon as he left the football game, he headed straight to the corner store. Jericho noticed him as he stepped out of the store with his six pack of beer inside of a brown paper bag. He hopped back in his car and they were right on his heels every step of the way as he headed home. He parked his car right in front of the house and went inside. Jericho parked up the street on the corner and quickly turned the headlights off. He picked up his cell phone to send a text message and awaited a response. All Jericho wanted to do now was wait long enough for Swift to be intoxicated and sleepy from drinking his beer before he attacked.

Earlier in the day, he got Gutta to send one of his young goons to break into Swift's apartment. They had him unlock the window in his bedroom because that was how they planned to enter the apartment. It was the easiest way for them to sneak up on him and catch him by surprise before he had a chance to get to his weapon to defend himself. If everything went as planned, they would be in and out in less than thirty minutes and Swift would no longer be an issue for Jericho.

"I trust you, Jericho. I know your skills are point. What the hell did he do to you anyway?"

"He's poking his nose where it doesn't belong. That's enough to get any man killed."

Jericho explained in detail the entire situation about the Marcus Harrison murder to Cesare. Once he got the full story of how Detective Swift was determined to not let the case go even though Geno got someone else to take the charge for Marcus' murder, Cesare fully understood Jericho's rationale for wanting to kill him. He too believed Marcus deserved to die for raping his sister, Shavon, and that no one should go to jail for it because it was a justifiable homicide. He thought Swift was being a prick for not letting the case go. He also remembered the slimy way he talked to him when he was interrogating him for Princess' murder. Taking all of this information into consideration, Cesare's mind was more at ease with what was about to go down. He felt Swift deserved his fate.

"You stay right here. I'll text you if the coast is clear for you to join me," Jericho instructed Cesare. He jumped out of the car and headed toward Swift's apartment. He had checked his watch and decided enough time had gone by and it was time for him to swing into action. Dressed in all black, he darted down the street en route to Swift's apartment. He glanced into his living room window and noticed Swift was fast asleep on the couch with a beer in his hand. He took out his phone to text

Cesare. Within two minutes, he had made his way from the car to join him. They quietly walked around to the other side of the house where Swift's bedroom was located. The window was ajar as planned and they both climbed inside. Jericho was armed with his trusty nickel plated 9mm Beretta while Cesare carried a fully loaded .38 special just as a precaution because Jericho rarely used guns to kill his victims.

When Jericho opened up Swift's bedroom door, he noticed he was still seated on the sofa fast asleep. He quickly crept up behind him and grabbed him around the neck in a choke hold. Swift awoke briefly to try and defend himself, but it was pointless. Jericho's grip was too tight for him to break free. Within a few seconds, he was out cold. Cesare helped him carry Swift's limp body into the bedroom so they could lay him across the bed. Jericho quickly undressed him down to his boxer shorts and got Cesare to help tie his arms and feet to his bedposts with the rope he had in his knapsack. By the time they were done, Swift began to awake from his slumber. When he opened his eyes, he was groggy and clueless as to how he wound up in his current predicament. He tried to break free, but the knots in the rope were too tight. When he saw Jericho and Cesare standing in front of him, his heart dropped in his chest.

"What the hell is going on? What kind of freaky shit is this? If you know what's good for you two, you better untie me now. I'm a cop for Christ's sake!" Swift rambled on. Jericho looked at Cesare and Cesare looked at him at the same time. They both burst out in laughter. The fact he was cop was a moot point right now.

"You just couldn't leave well enough alone, could you? You just had to keep snooping around and this is where your investigation winds up. You're tied up over there looking like a two dollar whore," Jericho joked adding insult to injury.

"Jericho, you've made a big mistake. I can promise you that for sure. I don't know what you have planned, but you won't get away with it. What is he doing here? Are you in on this too?" Swift asked when he glanced over at Cesare. Jericho grabbed a pair of socks out of Swift's dresser drawer and shoved them in his mouth. He had talked enough already. For the rest of the time he allowed him to live, he planned to be the last voice Swift would ever hear.

"We're family. You threaten one of us, you threaten all of us," Cesare replied boldly. His fear had vanished.

"Before I kill you, I'ma tell you everything you wanted to know so you can take it with you to your grave. We're all brothers. You see, our father had an affair with my mother and my sister and I were the result. As for the Marcus Harrison murder, he was killed by my girlfriend because he raped my sister. That bastard deserved to die for what he did. Geno got someone to take the charge for the case so we would be in the clear, but you had to play Inspector Gadget and not let things be. As a result, here we are. I hope I answered all of your questions. Your time is just about up," Jericho informed him without the slightest bit of regret. He reached into his pocket and pulled out a handful of pills. Jericho walked over to Swift, removed the sock from his mouth, and forcefully shoved the pills down his throat. He held his hand over his mouth so he couldn't spit them out. Once he was sure he had swallowed them, he shoved the sock back in his mouth.

"Jericho, what the hell are you doing?" Cesare asked totally confused.

"Just hold on for a few more minutes. It will all make sense," Jericho replied in a calm manner.

Cesare noticed how Jericho seemed to take pleasure in Swift's suffering. Swift tried to wiggle free from the ropes and to speak, but his efforts were futile. Almost on cue, Jericho received a text message on his phone. It was from China, a female associate he used on occasion for situations like this. He sent her a text in response and within a few minutes, they were startled when they heard a tapping sound from Swift's bedroom window.

Jericho instructed Cesare to go help China climb up into the apartment.

"Hey, baby girl, are you ready to earn your money?"Jericho asked her.

"You know it. I'm always ready to get paid," China replied.

Without any warning, she began to undress down to her bra and panties. She walked over to Swift's dresser drawer and took out one of his t-shirts to put on. She sat down at the foot of the bed. China was an integral part of Jericho's master plan. When Gutta snooped around Swift's apartment he came across nitrate medication in his bathroom which suggested Swift suffered from some form of cardiovascular disease. That was when Jericho came up with the idea of forcing Swift to ingest enough Viagra tablets to induce a heart attack which would kill him. That was where China came into the picture. Once Swift was dead, her job was to call the police and report that Swift passed out while they were about to have kinky sex. He wanted his death to look like an accident so there would be no police investigation.

"What the hell!!" Cesare yelled when he turned around.

He was freaked out when he saw Swift's entire body begin to shake uncontrollably. His breathing became heavy and within a few minutes, his eyes rolled into the back of his head. His body was totally still. Jericho walked over to him to check his pulse to confirm he was dead. He took his hand and closed Swift's eyelids. He began to untie the ropes around his arms and instructed Cesare to untie his feet. Once they were done, China climbed up in the bed and rolled around so that her DNA would be found in Swift's sheets.

"Jericho, you are either a psycho or a mad genius!" Cesare uttered. He had never experienced anything like this before in his life. He couldn't believe Jericho had a mind so diabolical to contrive such an intricate murder scheme.

"I tend to think I'm a little bit of both," he joked, but he was dead serious.

"What's next?" Cesare asked. He was ready to get the hell out of Swift's apartment and back home so he could process what just went down.

"Our job is done. China will handle the rest," he replied.

Jericho and Cesare exited out of the bedroom window and left China behind to finish the job. Cesare couldn't believe they just killed a police officer let alone did it without shedding an ounce of blood. He was also proud he kept his composure the entire time. Geno would be proud to know he stood tall like a Caprese man was supposed to do in these situations. Sal could never question his heart again. He put in work for his family. He was now officially one of them.

Chapter 16

It had been almost a week since Geno's release from prison. One of the conditions of his release on bail was he would have to be on house arrest and wear an ankle monitor. He was allowed to report to work, but had to return to his home by a set time each day. Given his looming legal situation, he was unable to see any of his clients. They were all reassigned to other attorneys at the law firm who were fully qualified to represent them more than adequately. Geno didn't complain about the restrictions imposed upon him by the court. He wrote it all off as a temporary inconvenience. Before he returned to work, he decided to take a few days off to relax with his family and get his head back in the game.

Gianna and Stefan were ecstatic to have him back where he belonged. During his brief hiatus from the office, Gianna and Stefan wanted to spend every waking moment with him. They missed his strong presence in the home dearly every day he was gone. They hugged and kissed on Geno so much, he barely had a moment to breathe, but he didn't mind it one bit. He missed them just as much. After his few days of rest came to an end, it was time for Geno to get back to the office and into the flow of things. He missed being hands on with running the company.

It was seven o'clock in the morning and he just finished having a healthy breakfast with Carina and the kids before he had to head into the office. He kissed both Gianna and Stefan on the cheek before Carina left to take them to school. After they were gone, he retreated to his home study to await Clay's arrival to drive him into the office.

While he sat in his study behind his desk, he pulled out an old photo album he kept throughout the years. It contained pictures of himself, his mother and father, and his three brothers when they were much younger. He thought about all of the fun they used to have together during those times with their fun filled family vacations. He became filled with deep emotions when he ran across a picture of him and Silvio together. At the time, they were in their early twenties and had a very close relationship. Geno sat and pondered to himself how things between the two of them went so wrong to the point he had to have his own brother killed. Given Silvio's plot against his life, he knew he had no choice but to do it if he wanted to survive, but it didn't make the pain he felt inside any less overwhelming at times. For better or worse, he was still his brother. He knew this was an act he would have to answer for on Judgment Day. Even though it was no compensation for Silvio's death, he was glad to have a solid relationship with Cesare and Jericho.

Geno's trip down memory lane was brought to an end when the buzzer on his intercom system went off to indicate Clay had arrived. He gathered up his belongings and headed to the front door. When he stepped outside, Clay already had the rear door to the Maybach open for him. He hopped in and they were on their way into the city. He already spoke with Jericho earlier in the morning. He had plans to meet with him as soon as he got in the office. They needed to discuss some pertinent business.

"We didn't have time to really talk the other day, Clay. What's new with you?"

"Nothing much, Geno, except I just bought me a new car and I'm thinking about asking my girl, Sicilia, to marry me," he replied.

"I must be paying you too much money, Mr. Big Spender. What kind of car did you get?"

"I just copped me a used Audi A6. It's five years old, but it's in mint condition. I got it for under fifteen grand. My payments are affordable. I remember what you told me about not being too flashy and living above my means," he replied. Geno was proud to know his words hadn't fallen upon deaf ears.

"The Audi is a nice car, kid. I like the way they handle on the road. I used to have an A8. It was a sweet ride. That's enough about your whip. What is this business about you saying you're getting married? How long have you known this girl?" Geno asked like a concerned parent.

"We've been dating for like six months now. I'm crazy about her. She has a good head on her shoulders. She's going to school to become a nurse," he answered.

"It's good to have a woman by your side who knows what she wants. Bring her by the house for dinner one night. I want Carina to check her out. We need to see if she's marriage material for you," Geno suggested.

"I will call her and set it up," he said eagerly. Geno's stamp of approval went a long way with Clay.

"What about you? What future plans do you have for yourself? I know you don't want to just live the rest of your life driving me around," Geno asked him.

Truth be told, the amount of money Geno paid him to be a driver was more than many middle class working citizens made on their jobs. Most of his time was spent however he chose to do so. All he had to do was be available whenever Geno needed him to take him somewhere. He had a sweet gig that most young men his age would die to have.

"I was thinking about enrolling in culinary school, Geno. I always wanted to be chef," Clay replied.

"Well, let's make that happen then. Get enrolled in school and get whatever educational requirements you need to get your license and then we can talk a little business about maybe opening up a restaurant for you one day. Remember one thing kid: never be satisfied being a worker. Always strive to become your own Boss," Geno advised him. He was always in the market for a new business venture to invest in.

"Yes sir, I'm on it," Clay stated excitedly. He arrived at Geno's office faster than he thought he would. He double parked the car in front of the building and walked around to open the door for Geno.

"Make sure you keep your phone on, Clay. As a matter of fact, hang around downtown for a while. I may not be at the office for too long today," Geno instructed him. Clay nodded his head to acknowledge his request. Geno stepped away from the car and headed toward the building. He looked up and saw Jericho standing by the front door. He walked over in his direction. They both reached out and embraced one another. It was the first time they saw each other since Geno got released from jail.

"It's good to see you, Geno. I'm glad you got out of the hell hole."

"Tell me about it. I'm glad to be home. We have a lot to talk about. Let's go inside."

The two men made their way into the building and up to Geno's office. When Geno got off the elevator, he was greeted by a loud round of applause from his staff. They were happy to have him back at work. As he made his way down the hallway, he stuck his head into Jia's office. She was happy to see him. She got up from her seat to give him a hug.

"I'm glad your back, Geno. You were missed around here," Jia stated honestly. She looked up at Jericho and spoke to him as well.

"Give me like 30 minutes and stop by my office so we can talk," Geno told her. She agreed to do so. He made his way to his office and went inside. Jericho walked in right behind him and closed the door.

"Before we get to the Sam Bradford situation, I need to put you up on another situation I had to handle before it got out of hand. It has to do with the cop involved with that little problem you worked on for me," Jericho stated obviously speaking in code in reference to Detective Swift. He ran down the whole story to Geno and awaited his response.

"I can certainly understand why you couldn't wait on me to fix that situation again for you without having to resort to such extreme measures. Clearly he was intent on making a problem for both of us. You did what you had to do and it's a done deal. I can't believe you made the poor fool OD on Viagra though. That is hilarious. So, how did Cesare hold up? Do you think he's ready for this other thing?" Geno asked

"He was a little shaky at first, but he held his own. I think he'll be fine," Jericho answered.

"That's good to hear. Where are we at with this other thing?" Geno asked about their plan for Sam Bradford.

"Your intel was good money. Surprisingly, the Feds have yet to move him to another location. The security they have around him is tight, but nothing my guys can't handle. I've got my crew in place and I'm ready to move on this ASAP," Jericho replied.

"You've got the green light. I want it to be bloody. This needs to make national news, but it can't come back on me in anyway," Geno stated bluntly.

"You don't have to say anything else. The situation is handled. Since we've got that out of the way, Geno, I wanted to bend your ear for a minute about your man Sal," Jericho stated.

"What about Sal? Is there a problem?" Geno inquired. He repositioned himself in his seat so he could focus his attention on what Jericho had to say.

Jericho wasn't sure how Geno would take what he had to say about his right hand man, but he needed to get it off of his chest. Never the bashful type, he proceeded to tell him about his observations about Sal's behavior toward him as well as Jia. Jericho normally didn't butt in other people's business, but he was extra sensitive to the Jia situation after what happened to Shavon. Geno listened attentively to everything Jericho said without saying a word in return.

"Thanks for bringing all of that to my attention," Geno stated stoically. Jericho wasn't sure what to make of Geno's short response to what he just told him. He was a hard man to read.

"I've gotta run. I've got some things to do," Jericho responded.

"Hey, tell my girl Nina I said to take it easy. She's carrying my nephew. That's precious cargo right there. I'm happy for you two. When this is all over with, we need together just the four of us," Geno suggested.

"Thanks. I'll tell her what you said. That sounds like a plan."

Geno got up to walk Jericho to the door. They shook hands and Jericho was on his way. Geno saw Jia walking down the hall. They made eye contact. He motioned for her to come into his office. Sal happened to be walking by at the same time. Geno took note of the uncomfortable look on her face when she passed by him. Nonetheless, Jia stopped what she was doing and did as he requested. When she walked into his office, she noticed Geno had a very serious look on his face.

"Jia, is there something you need to tell me about Sal?" Geno asked her rather directly before she even had a chance to sit down.

"What do you mean?" she shot back at him nervously.

"Jia, let's not play games. You should know me well enough to know you can come to me about anything," Jericho stated to try and ease her anxiety.

"I don't want to cause any problems, Geno. I just want to do my job," Jia replied.

"Okay, let me be more specific. Did Sal put his hands on you in a way that made you feel uncomfortable? It's a yes or no question!" he stated angrily.

"Yes, he tried to force himself on me. He told me if I told you he would hurt me and Solomon," she admitted.

"Did he really say that? You don't have to worry about a thing. Don't say a word about this to anyone, do you hear me?"

"Yes, I hear you, Geno. I'm sorry you have to deal with something like this with all of the things you've been through lately," she replied.

"Jia, you have nothing to apologize for because you did nothing wrong. In fact, I'm sorry I yelled at you. I was upset. You shouldn't have to go through being sexually harassed at work. Sal should know better. I'll deal with him. He won't be a problem for you anymore," Geno reassured her.

"Thank you, Geno," she replied. She felt a sense of relief. If Geno told her not to worry, then she wouldn't. He was a man of his word. Jia got up and headed back to her office. She felt like a heavy burden had been lifted from her shoulders.

Jia's version of what transpired confirmed what Jericho just told him. Geno was hot. Sal's behavior was unacceptable, especially as it related to Jia. She was a valuable member of his team. Geno would not tolerate a man disrespecting a woman in that manner especially one associated with his name and brand. With all of his own drama he had to deal with as far as his court case, he couldn't believe Sal would add on to his list of issues by being so reckless. Geno didn't want his emotional response to the situation to ruin a lifelong friendship. As a result, he wanted to sit on this issue for a minute before he approached Sal. How he handled him could have residual ramifications he had to be sure he was prepared to face.

Chapter 17

It was around ten o'clock at night and it appeared to be just another cool fall evening. The temperature was in the forty degree range, but the wind chill factor made it seem colder. The rainfall had been steady all day long. It made for a slippery commute for drivers on their journeys to and from work. The rain, combined with the dense fog, made for the perfect night to be at home in the bed sleep. For Jericho, it was the prime time for him to execute the perfect murder.

Jericho and Gutta decided to meet at another one of his homes in Baltimore County. Cesare rode along with him. This particular house was where Gutta stashed a gang of weapons and ammunition for situations like this. He used this house as a meeting point to plan out many of his biggest robberies. He had a safe filled with an undisclosed amount of money and fake travel papers hidden behind a steel reinforced secret wall in the master bedroom. Gutta believed a man in his line of work couldn't have enough options available if he needed a place to lay low for a spell if it was hot out in the streets.

"This seems like old times, doesn't it Jericho? I remember the first time I took you out on a job. You were a scared little motherfucker, but you held your own. Once you got your first kill, there was no turning back. Look at you now. You're a certified killing machine," Gutta reminisced about his prize student. Jericho had now become a master with skills that matched, if not surpassed, his own. He quickly inserted a forty round magazine clip into his AK-47.

Gutta truly missed being in the thick of the action with Jericho. He could trust him to be on point and to watch his back at all times. Ever since he went to work for Geno, things weren't the same for Gutta. They formed an unbeatable team together for a lot of years out in the streets. They pulled off a gang of successful robberies and contract killings without ever going to jail, unlike some of their other partners in crime. However, it was about more than just the jobs they pulled off. Jericho was like a little brother to him. He represented the closest thing to family he had.

Without Jericho around as much, Gutta felt depressed at times. Yet, in still, he was genuinely happy to see Jericho attempting to make a better life for him and Nina. With all the hard times he suffered through in his life, he deserved to find some inner peace. When Jericho told him about Nina being pregnant, Gutta knew his good friend made the right decision to make a change in his life. This one last job would give him the financial security to live the comfortable type of life that Gutta let go of ever having many years ago. He had resolved himself to being an outlaw until they put him six feet deep.

"Yeah, you taught me a lot, Gutta. We've had some close calls and laid down a lot of bodies along the way, but this job right here will be the toughest of them all. We can't afford to make not even the slightest of a mistake," Jericho reiterated to him. He too missed Gutta's comradery, but he also grew to accept that life was about choices and accepting the consequences for those choices. While he and Gutta now followed distinctly different paths, they would forever be bonded by their history together. No standup soldier could ever totally abandon his comrades in battle.

"That's why you've got me in this with you, partner," Gutta reminded him how he was just as efficient and effective as Jericho at getting the job done with no hiccups along the road.

Jericho's weapon of choice tonight was his customized Heckler and Koch G36. He also had his trusty 9mm Glock strapped to his waistline as a backup. He armed Cesare with a Mossberg 12 gauge shotgun. For the past week, he took him out to a private shooting range and gave him a crash course on how to use it properly. Cesare surprisingly was a fast learner and pretty accurate shooter for a novice.

Jericho charged Gutta with assembling the rest of their crew. He put together a team of nine of the most cold hearted soldiers he could find. He personally vouched for them being the type of fearless men they needed for this job. There was no room for cowardice or trepidation in this unit. Everybody had to pull their own weight. Adding in Gutta, Cesare, and Jericho, this twelve man team was ready to go to war. Gutta had them all armed with the most lethal firepower he could find. They all had on body armor suits as an added measure of protection.

For the past week, Gutta and Jericho cased out the remote area where the house the Feds had Sam Bradford stashed away was located. They had to make sure their attack would be surgical and precise. If they got caught killing a federal agent or a federal witness, they would all definitely get the gas chamber. After careful observation, they had the daily routines of Sam's security detail down to a science.

Because of the level of danger involved with the job, Geno spared no expense for this dangerous mission. He agreed to pay Jericho five million dollars in cash once it was done. Jericho arranged to pay Gutta one million dollars and to split another two million dollars between Cesare and the rest of their crew. After they were all paid, that would leave Jericho's share of the bounty at a cool two million dollars. That was more than enough money to make any man consider the job, but not just any man could get it done. Jericho possessed the mental focus and expertise to make it happen. Gutta had no problem whatsoever taking orders from Jericho for this caper. He trained him well to take command like a general in times like this. He placed his full confidence in him to make this a successful mission.

"Cesare, how are you feeling brother? Are you ready for this?" Jericho asked.

"I'm ready for whatever. Let's get it done," Cesare replied. There were no signs of fear in his voice or in his outward appearance. He was ready to prove how much of a soldier he was to his brothers.

Jericho glanced over at Sarge and Banks. They both were in their mid fifties, but in excellent physical shape. They were two highly decorated soldiers who saw combat action with Gutta in Vietnam so he knew they were mentally equip for this type of action. Sarge busied himself sharpening up his hunting knife while Banks gave his weapon one final thorough cleaning. The rest of the squad checked their firearms as well to make sure everything was on point. Jericho and Gutta exchanged a few final words to confirm they were on the same page with everything. With all of their ducks in a row, it was time to get to work. Jericho rallied up the troops and they hopped inside of the two stolen vans one by one. As they drove down the road, there was a deafening silence in the air. There was no need for any more words. It was time for some action.

Chapter 18

It was a little past eleven o'clock in the evening. Agent Gelasco was fast asleep on the couch with his mouth wide open. A steady flow of drool spilled out of the side of his mouth onto the small pillow that he rested his head on. His loud snoring echoed throughout the entire house. It was so loud it forced Agent Mancini to turn the volume to the television up as high as it could go just to drown the noise out. Mancini wished he could stuff a sock up both of his nostrils to shut him up, but he resisted the temptation to do so. He and Gelasco were not only partners on the job, but they were the best of friends. On their off time, they went on weekend hunting and fishing trips together. Their wives and children hung out together as well while they spent long hours on the job. They both also shared a mutual interest in wanting to rid the streets of as many criminal elements as they possibly could.

Mayhem just recently decided to increase security for his star witness. He had two more agents stationed outside in front of the home in a patrol car as well as two agents on post in a car parked in the rear driveway. He needed for Sam to stay alive long enough to testify against Geno, but after that, whatever happened to him really didn't matter. Sam was just like any other criminal to Mayhem. He broke the law and sought to make a deal to get out of serving time in prison. He didn't view him any differently than he did Geno. He had no respect for him as a man at all. He was just a pawn he used to get the bigger fish he so desperately wanted to capture.

Since he couldn't find anything to watch on television, Mancini decided to make a trip upstairs to check on Sam. He was sure he would either find Sam on the toilet once again taking a dump or in the bed tossing and turning because he couldn't sleep. Everything Sam did was predictable. Mancini made his way up the stairs and walked toward the master bedroom. When he opened the door, the lights were off but the television was on and tuned to an infomercial about some magical pills for penis enlargement. Sam was seated on the edge of the bed with his head hung low sobbing like a baby.

"Sam, what the hell are you crying for now?" he asked. Mancini saw this same song and dance from him countless times before. He shook his head in disgust at the sight of this poor excuse for a man.

"I messed up. I really messed up my life. I can't believe I did this to myself. My mother would be ashamed of the man I have become. I disappointed my wife and my kids," he babbled on. His words were partially incoherent due to the glob of saliva lodged in his throat. Mancini saw his attempt to throw a pity party for himself to be totally over the top, but he decided to indulge him for a spell.

"Pull yourself together, Sam. You've got to suck it up. You should be proud of yourself. You made a bad mistake and now you're doing something to try and make it right. Helping us put Geno Caprese away is a step in the right direction. If we're able to also nab Manuel Lopez too, then that's even more good news," he tried to reason with him.

In his line of work, Mancini not only was a federal agent, but he also had to play the role of a counselor and friend at times. He had to be that comforting ear an informant needed in moments like this. Whatever it took to convince them to testify in court, he did what was necessary.

"I don't want to testify now. I've changed my mind. Geno was always fair with me. He never did me wrong. We made a lot of money together. He never cheated me out of a dime. It's wrong for me to send him to jail. I can't do this! I can't do this!" he stated over and over.

"Sam, listen to me my friend. You're just nervous. You can and will do this. Geno Caprese is a cold blooded gangster. He sells drugs. He has people killed for not going along with his wishes. He is not a good guy. He is the devil. Think about all of the lives ruined by the drugs he puts out on the streets. You see the news. You see all of the crack babies and heroin addicted mothers in Baltimore City strung out on his dope. You'll be doing the world a favor to get him off the streets," he reasoned with him.

"This is all hard for me. I've never been to jail before. I went to college and got a degree. I'm not built for this street life. I should just kill myself," he threatened.

"Now you're talking like a fool. Think about your wife and children. They need you, man. Once this is all over, you'll have a new life somewhere far away from here. You're kind of lucky if you really think about it a little deeper. Just imagine how many people wish they could get a fresh start in life like you're about to do," Mancini said to further solidify his position on the matter.

While he was in the middle of his conversation with Sam, Mancini was startled by the sound of gunfire outside of the residence. The sound was so loud he couldn't tell if it were coming from the front or the rear of the house. Sam ran into the bathroom and locked the door. Gelasco glanced out of the bedroom window and saw the two agents out in front of the house engaged in an all out gun battle with several masked men dressed in all black. The car they were in was riddled with bullets. When he saw the agent on the driver's side fall down in the street, he knew he was dead. The other agent continued to fire his weapon in response to the masked team of assassins before he too was killed. Mancini ran downstairs to check on his partner. When he got downstairs, Gelasco was already awake and positioned at the front window with his gun in hand returning fire.

"What the hell is going on?" Mancini yelled.

"It's an ambush! I already called for backup!" Gelasco replied. He ducked down behind the couch to take cover from the incoming bullets.

The sounds of gunfire from the front and rear of the home continued to echo loudly through the normally quiet neighborhood. It sounded like the fourth of July. Gelasco came from behind the couch again and crawled over to the front window. When he raised his gun to return fire, he managed to duck down just quickly enough to not get hit by the bullets that raced past his head. When he heard a break in the gunfire, he jumped up and let off a few more rounds from his service revolver through the front window. He was almost out of bullets and couldn't wait for backup to arrive.

Mancini managed to make it to the front door. When he opened it, he was greeted by a hail of bullets that made the door look like a slice of Swiss cheese. Two of the bullets struck him in his upper torso and he fell to the floor. Blood leaked from his wounds. Gelasco crawled over to where he was at to see how bad he was injured.

"I'm not going to make it, partner. Sam is hiding in the bathroom. You know what to do," Mancini stated before he lost consciousness and crossed over to the other side. Gelasco didn't even have a chance to defend himself when he looked up and saw Jericho's rifle pointed at his head from the doorway. There were several armed men standing right behind him.

"Where is he?" Jericho barked at Gelasco.

"Where is who? I don't know who he is," Gelasco stated defiantly. A few seconds later, the back door was kicked in. This was a clear indication all of the other agents were dead and he was the last man left. Gelasco dropped his gun and raised his arms to surrender.

"I'm only asking you one more time. Where is he?" Jericho asked again.

"I'm not telling you shit. Help is on the way. All of you bastards are gonna die. I would advise you to get out of here while you still can," he replied. He was determined to stick to his guns. Gelasco refused to give up a federal witness under any circumstances. He had already accepted he was about to die. He planned to go out on his shield.

"Have it your way. Good night motherfucker," Jericho uttered before he took his 9mm Glock from his waist and unleashed several rounds of gunfire directly aimed at Gelasco's face. He would definitely have to have a closed casket funeral.

"Let's check the whole house. He's in here somewhere. We need to hurry up and get this done!" Gutta screamed.

All of the men spread out to search the house. As he made his way up the steps, Gutta felt something warm on the back of his neck. He reached his hand around to check it out and discovered he was bleeding. He had been hit by a bullet in the gun battle they had with the agents stationed outside.

"Are you okay?" Jericho asked with sincere concern. Neither one of them had ever took a bullet before.

"I'm good. Let's get this done," Gutta responded. Even though he was wounded, he soldiered on. He had a job to do. He could patch up his wound later.

"I found him! He's in the bedroom!" Cesare yelled from the upper level of the house. He found Sam curled up under the bed shaking like a leaf. Jericho and Gutta raced toward the master bedroom. Cesare stood over top of Sam with his weapon in his hand. He waited for Jericho to give him the word to end his life.

"Please don't kill me! Tell Geno I'm sorry! Please have mercy on me! I won't testify in court! I don't wanna die like this!" Sam begged and pleaded.

"You're a worthless piece of shit. You ratted on my brother to save your own ass. You can see now the Feds couldn't even save your ass from us. You should've just come to Geno when you got pinched. He would've helped you out. Instead, you chose to switch sides," Cesare ranted on. He was amped up off of the adrenaline rush.

"We don't have time for all of that talking, Cesare. Put his ass to sleep," Jericho ordered him.

Cesare raised his gun to shoot him, but Jericho stopped him before he pulled the trigger. He reached on to his waistband and handed him his knife. He took his hand and ran it across his neck to indicate how Geno wanted Sam to die. This murder was personal and designed to send a message. Cesare hesitated for a second before he took the knife from Jericho's hand. He bent down and sliced Sam's throat from ear to ear just like he was told to do. Blood gushed out everywhere. They all stood and watched Sam choke on his own blood while he took his last breath.

"Let's get outta here!" Jericho yelled to his troops.

They all ran down the stairs and exited the house as fast as they could. They hopped back in the vans and exited the scene. They were all supposed to meet back up at Gutta's house. While Sarge drove the van they were in, Jericho was in the back with Gutta. He checked out his bullet wound to see how bad it was. He noticed it was still bleeding heavily.

"We need to get you to a doctor, Gutta."

"Man, I don't need a damn doctor. This is nothing. I'm fine. Just get me back to the meeting point and I'll pluck this bullet out and stitch it up myself."

"Are you sure, Gutta?"

"Listen to me, youngblood; I know what I'm doing. Don't forget I'ma war veteran. Tell the truth, Jericho, it felt good to be in the mix again, didn't it?"

"Yeah, I'm not gonna lie, it did."

"Your brother Cesare sliced that fool from ear to ear like it was nothing. That boy is a natural at this. He didn't even flinch."

Jericho glanced up at Cesare. He noticed something different about him. He appeared to be extremely relaxed for a man that just committed his first murder. In fact, he looked as though he was relieved and anxious to do it again.

"Cesare, you did good, man. You did real good."

"That bastard had to die. I would do it again if somebody threatened anybody in our family."

Cesare was unrepentant for his actions. In fact, he was quite proud. Jericho and Gutta both recognized the glare he had in his eyes. They both had that look before and knew it well. It was the look one had when he no longer feared dying, but got a thrill out of causing death. That feeling of power from having another man's fate in his hands began to race through Cesare's veins. Killing Sam awakened a side to him he never knew existed. Jericho hoped he didn't regret what he just allowed him to do because Cesare would be headed down a very dark path with an unpredictable ending. On the long ride to Gutta house, they all dozed off to sleep. They were awakened when Sarge hit a bump in the road as he turned off the road and made his way up to the house.

"Oh shit! Gutta, wake up man! Wake up! Wake up! I need you to wake up!" Jericho yelled hysterically.

He glanced over at Gutta and shined his flashlight in his direction. He noticed his face looked a little pale and knew that wasn't a good sign. He reached over to check his pulse and found none. He shook him several times, but he didn't respond. Tears welled up in Jericho's eyes. His big brother, his partner in crime, and mentor was dead. He pounded his hands on the sides of the van to let out his anger. Cesare grabbed onto him to console him. Gutta lived his life the way he wanted to and he went out with bang just like he would have wanted to do. They carried his body out of the back of the van. Jericho planned to bury him on his property and have a brief ceremony for him. Gutta's restless soul could now eternally fly free and wreak havoc in the Hereafter.

Chapter 19

It was three o'clock in the morning when Mayhem was awakened out of his sleep by the ringing sound of his cell phone. He felt around on his nightstand for his glasses. He accidentally knocked them on the floor. He got up out of the bed as fast as his middle aged body would allow him to do to retrieve them. Once he secured them on his eyes, he glanced at his phone to see who had called him at this ungodly hour and robbed him of some much needed rest. His wife, Olivia, was still fast asleep totally oblivious to his current struggle. He didn't recognize the number in his call log, but he still pressed "Send" to redial the number.

"Mr. Mayhem, this is homicide detective Prescott. I'm calling you because we have a serious problem. There has been an incident involving several federal agents and your primary witness in the Geno Caprese case," the detective informed him.

"What kind of incident? What the hell is going on?" he yelled into the phone. The loud tone of his voice startled Olivia. She turned around to see what the commotion was all about.

"We've been informed by the Prince George County police department that your witness and all of the federal agents are dead. Whoever did this was a monster. There was blood everywhere, Sir. This was a massacre designed to send a message," Detective Prescott theorized.

"Holy Mother of Jesus, this can't be happening. Somebody please wake me up. This has to be a nightmare. Send a car here to get me now. I need to see the crime scene. I need to see this for myself!" Mayhem yelled into the phone. He pounded his fist on the bed. He stood up and walked back and forth across the floor in a manic state. His face turned blush red.

"We already have a car on the way, Sir," Prescott told him before he heard the dial tone.

Mayhem, in a fit of rage, rudely hung up the phone in Prescott's ear. He wasn't thinking clearly given the circumstances. He couldn't believe what he just heard. His dream case against Geno just went up in smoke. Sam Bradford, his star witness, was dead. There were six dead federal agents who also died connected to this case. He knew he would have to come up with an explanation as to how this happened on his watch. The media circus he would face had just begun. Everything that could go wrong had gone wrong. Mayhem didn't know what to do or say. This type of public relations nightmare would surely reach all the way up to the U.S. Attorney General's office. His entire career was on the line because somebody had to take the fall for this mess and he appeared to be the prime candidate. Mayhem found a burst of energy and managed to get dressed in record time. He sat down on the side of the bed to put on his shoes. He cursed out loud because he had a hard time tying his shoes due to his bad nerves. Olivia just observed her husband in such a frantic state.

"Gavin, what is going on with you? Where do you think you're going?" she asked him.

"He's done it again, honey. He's done it to me again. I had him right where I wanted him and he has somehow managed to find a way to squirm his way out of my grasp," Mayhem ranted on and on like a madman. He paced back and forth across the floor for several minutes mumbling to himself before he sat back down on the bed. He held his face in his hands. He was beyond frustrated as he had every right to be.

"What on God's Earth are you talking about?" she asked still puzzled by his erratic behavior.

"Geno Caprese is who I'm talking about. He killed my witness against him as well as the agents I had protecting him. They're all dead because of me. I'm going to lose my job for this mess."

In just a split second, it all became clear to Olivia. She knew the name Geno Caprese too well. She could never forget the low down dirty dog that broke her daughter's heart and almost ruined her life. She had a front row seat over the years as she watched her husband become obsessed with getting revenge against him.

"Baby, it's time to let this thing go. You are losing your mind over this Geno thing. I hate him just as much as you do, but going through all of this over one criminal is not worth the hassle. I see how you stress yourself out. Yes, he did our daughter wrong, but it's time to move on. Amy has put her life back together so there is no need to continue to rehash things from the past. Plus, hearing all of this talk about agents and witnesses being killed lets me know how far out of hand this thing between you and Geno has gotten. I don't want to lose you behind this foolishness," she attempted to reason with him.

"I hear what you're saying, honey, but this is not foolishness. I took an oath to put villains like Geno behind bars and now my whole career is on the line because I tried to do the right thing," he argued.

"Yes, you did take an oath to uphold the law, but you also took an oath to me as your wife," she replied.

"I don't know what else to say. I have to see this thing through to the end. I have no choice at this point, honey," he stated resolutely.

Olivia's pleas fell upon deaf ears. He was determined to find a way to get Geno off of the streets. Mayhem walked over to the window to glance outside. He saw a police car headed up his driveway. He tried to kiss Olivia on the cheek, but she extended out her hand to block his lips from touching her. Mayhem made his way downstairs and out the door. He needed to see firsthand the carnage he knew Geno caused. He hoped and prayed there would be evidence at the scene or a witness that could tie Geno to this heinous act. If not, all of his efforts to convict Geno were in vain.

His ride to the crime scene took close to an hour. Along the way, he thought about his wife's words to him. He knew she was right about letting his grudge against Geno go, but he was too stubborn and set in his ways to heed her advice. His obsession with Geno led him to do the unthinkable. For his entire legal career, his peers respected him for being a stand up, by the book kind of guy who did things the right way. Never would he have imagined in a million years he would find himself paying off a judge to keep a defendant locked up in jail, but his hatred for Geno led him down that road.

He reminisced about his long journey through law school and how proud his parents felt when he passed the bar exam. He thought about the first case he prosecuted as a young attorney and all of his many major victories throughout the years. It was a shame such a brilliant legal career was about to be tainted because of one case. However, this was the hand he had currently and he had to play it until the bitter end however it turned out. Mayhem wasn't the kind of man to run away from his responsibilities. If this mishap required him to fall on his shield and take the full blame for this mess, then that was exactly what he planned to do.

The rivalry between him and Geno wasn't just about Amy. In fact, she had even went as far as to suggest to her father he should let his grudge against Geno go because she had moved on with her life and was happy now, but he didn't listen. Their rivalry had more to do with his ego and his frustration with seeing Geno always win cases by bending the rules while he won or loss cases by sticking to the letter of the law. He felt he deserved the praise and accolades Geno received because he believed he was the more honorable and morally upright man between the two of them. Add in the fact they were both Alpha males, there would be no end to their rivalry unless one of them caved in and decided to surrender to the other. That was unlikely to happen. They were too much alike to admit this feud was pointless and caused a lot of pain and suffering to those around him.

When he arrived on the crime scene, Mayhem stepped out of the squad car. He walked right through the swarming crowd of media hounds to survey the scene. He couldn't believe what he saw. There were blood and shell casings all over the streets. He saw the bullet riddled bodies of the federal agents in the front and rear of the home and almost puked. He was consumed with feelings of guilt at the sight of Sam with his throat slit so badly his head was almost severed from his neck. It scene reminded him of the images he saw of the Nicole Brown Simpson murder scene. Never had Mayhem witnessed such a lack of regard for human life. He wondered to himself had he gone too far with Geno. Even if he did, it was too late to turn back now. The damage had been done. Once he saw all he needed to see, he walked back to the squad car and got inside without making a statement to the press. There was nothing he could say to fix this situation. Mayhem headed to his office to prepare his next move.

Chapter 20

Geno had his alarm clock set for six o'clock in the morning. When he heard it go off, he reached over to his nightstand to shut off the annoying sound so it wouldn't wake up Carina. She needed her rest because she was exhausted from the mind bending sex they had the night before. Geno grabbed the remote control so he could turn the television on. He turned the television to the Fox morning news. A broad smile came across his face when the story he wanted to hear came on.

Geno listened carefully to the news anchor tell the gruesome tale about the murder of six federal agents and a federal witness just outside of the nation's capital. Jericho had delivered the bloodbath he promised. While he and Cesare were out committing murder, Geno was at home making passionate love to his beautiful wife, Carina. She, along with his ankle monitor and the security cameras positioned all around his home, provided him with an airtight alibi that could be verified easily.

With Sam Bradford now dead and unable to testify against him, it was now up to Geno and Solomon to do their part to make this matter go away for good. Geno knew it was just a matter of time before the Feds came and tried to arrest him for this brutal massacre. He would obviously be their prime suspect in the case. He clearly had a motive to want Sam dead, but the burden of proof was on the government to establish how he had the opportunity to hatch such a vicious attack given his restricted mobility being on house arrest. Geno intentionally sent his children to spend the weekend with his mother so they wouldn't have to see him carted off to jail again. He had already thoroughly prepared Carina for what was about to go down. She had a role to play in his master plan as well. He coached her on exactly what she needed to do to play her part.

With Carina still sleep, Geno got up to take a shower. The fresh, warm water up against his flesh enlivened his soul. He fully appreciated being able to shower at home alone in his own bathroom as opposed to in a prison shower with a gang of other men. His prison experience got him to thinking even more seriously about his future and some changes he needed to make in his life to avoid ever going back there again once this was all said and done. He valued his freedom more than the boatloads of money he made from his many business ventures. He decided it was time for him to close the door on all of his illegal activities and to go totally legit because it just wasn't in him anymore to face the consequences that came along with the money he made from the streets. He knew Sal and Milton would be upset with his decision, but his mind was made up. If they chose to continue to indulge in the street life, then that was on them. While he enjoyed his shower, he was startled when he looked up to see Carina walking toward him through the thick steam that totally engulfed the bathroom. Her nakedness got a rise out of him instantly.

"Can I join you in there?"

"You absolutely can join me. Come on in here now."

Carina stepped inside of the shower and positioned herself up against the shower wall. Geno bent down and kissed her square in the mouth. The taste of his tongue inside of her mouth made Carina's legs get weak. She grabbed a hold of him and wrapped her legs around his waist. Geno skillfully inserted himself inside of her. That initial feeling from his penetration made her butt cheeks tighten up. She bounced up and down on his manhood with her arms draped across his shoulders. Geno placed his hands on the shower wall to maintain his balance. He used all five of his senses to help him deliver pleasure to her over and over. To hear her scream his name and to see her facial expressions when she did it made Geno ramp up the pace of his pelvic thrusts. His sense of taste was titillated when he pressed his mouth up against her breasts and sucked on her nipples. He loved the sweet raspberry scent of her hair as it brushed up against his nostrils. His hands explored her body and wound up firmly attached to her waist when he pulled her closer to him. The emotional energy between them was intense. In a matter of ten minutes, they both managed to satisfy each other mentally and physically.

"Step out of the shower now with your hands raised in the air!" a voice yelled at them.

They were interrupted out of their moment of bliss when the door to the bathroom was kicked open and a herd of police officers, with their weapons drawn, rushed inside. Carina screamed out loud like she was surprised even though Geno already told her they would be coming at some point today to arrest him. However, he wished they would have at least waited until she was fully clothed before they invaded her home. Carina noticed several of the officers lustfully eyeing her curvy figure up and down. She shot them all a dirty look while she grabbed a towel off of the rack to cover herself up.

"What the hell is going on? Have you people lost your minds barging in on me and my wife like this? I will have all of your badges for this invasion of my privacy!" Geno threatened while he and Carina followed their orders. They both had their hands raised above their heads while they walked out of the bathroom.

"Geno Caprese, you are under arrest for conspiracy to commit multiple murders," he was informed by the lead officer, Sergeant Macon.

"You can't take my husband away! He didn't kill anybody! This is a mistake!" Carina screamed hysterically. She put on the dramatic performance of a lifetime playing the role of the traumatized wife just as Geno instructed her to do.

"Mrs. Caprese, I understand this situation is awkward for you, but I need you to please calm down," Sergeant Macon calmly advised her.

"Calm down? You people are harassing my husband and you want me to calm down? You burst into my home and violate my privacy, but you want me to calm down? How would you feel if I came into your house while you were being intimate with your wife? Calm down? Why don't you go to hell?" Carina replied with pure venom in her tone.

"I understand where you're coming from, Mrs. Caprese, but your husband is facing serious charges here," he tried to reason with her. He clearly felt awkward with the whole situation. He truly hated when wives and children were dragged into the situation when he went to arrest a suspect. However, it happened all of the time and there was not much he could do about it at this point.

"Baby, calm down and just do what the officer says. I'll be alright. I know I didn't kill anybody so I'm not worried at all. This is all a part of the game Mayhem is playing with me, but he messed up this time. Officer, can I at least put some clothes on?" Geno turned and asked him in a humble tone. He was still naked with his manhood fully exposed.

"You've got five minutes to throw something on. Make it quick!" Sergeant Macon barked at him.

Geno quickly ran into his closet to grab a pair of jeans and a shirt to put on. He grabbed a pair of sneakers from his shoe rack to put on his feet. Once he was fully dressed, he was placed in handcuffs. The officers led him out of the bedroom and down the stairs. The first time when the Feds came to arrest him Geno was caught off guard, but this time he was fully prepared. He winked at Carina as he was carted away. He couldn't wait to get to the police station so that he and Mayhem could have another chance to engage in a high stakes game of mental chess. He planned to come out on top this time. Geno closed his eyes and visualized the entire scenario as it played out in his head. A smile came across his face because the ball was now back in his court. Mayhem had no clue what lied ahead for him.

Chapter 21

When he reached the police station, Geno was placed in an interrogation room, but he wasn't in there alone for long. Solomon arrived not more than ten minutes after he did. Geno had already arranged for Carina to call Solomon so that he could meet him at the police station. While the two men waited for Geno to be questioned by the police officers, they discussed their strategy. Geno filled Solomon in on his plan and how he expected for things to play out. Once Geno was done, Solomon simply sat with his mouth open. He couldn't believe all of what he just heard from his boss.

"Geno, I just don't know what to say. How do you come up with this stuff?" Solomon asked curiously.

"It takes years of practice to get to the place I'm in my legal career, Solomon. In addition, you have to be willing to swim with sharks if you want to become a big fish in this town. Every man has a weak spot no matter how upright or moral he appears to be. We all have skeletons in our closet. It takes a shrewd and patient man to uncover those weaknesses and he also has to have the balls to use them to his advantage. Nothing that I'm doing is unique or hasn't been done before. I've just learned from the best and become a master at this. Sit back and learn a thing or two from me, young man," Geno replied rather cockily.

Geno's full swagger was on display. His brief lesson to Solomon was cut short when Mayhem walked into the room. Normally a homicide detective interrogated a suspect, but Mayhem pulled rank on the lead detective. He wanted to question Geno himself, just as Geno expected him to do. This case was too major for him not to do so. The mean look on Mayhem's face indicated he was all about business and not in the mood for small talk.

"Just tell me how you did it, Geno? How did you manage to kill him and all of my men? Look at these pictures. You are a monster!" Mayhem blurted out angrily. He threw the photos on the table for Geno to view. He glanced at them briefly before he quickly closed the folders back up. Geno crossed his legs and composed himself before he decided to speak.

"Mayhem, you need to calm down. I have no clue what you're talking about with this nonsense here. I did not kill Sam or those agents. I had nothing to do with that at all. I didn't find out about any of this until I saw it on the news this morning," Geno lied.

"That's bullshit and you know it, Geno. You did this to save your own ass, but it's not going to work. You're going down for these murders, you arrogant son of a bitch!" Mayhem yelled.

"I will say it again so you hear me clearly: I did not do this. I'm not your guy for this one and I will not allow you to railroad me into a conviction. Yes, it's true I did think Sam deserved to die for being a rat, but I'm not crazy enough to kill him and a bunch of federal agents. That's insane. I've been a lot of things in my life, but a lunatic is not one of them," Geno attempted to reason with him.

Mayhem didn't buy his innocence act. He became more enraged with every word Geno spoke. His breathing became heavy. He banged his fist on the table. He was too upset to even wince from the pain it caused him. Unable to control himself any longer, he jumped across the table and wrapped his hands around Geno's throat. Solomon instinctively jumped up to pull him off of his client, but Mayhem's grip was too tight. Geno maintained his composure and did his best to appear shocked by Mayhem's attempt to manhandle him. If he wanted to, he could've got Mayhem off of him, but chose not to do so. Mayhem played right into his plot and did exactly what he hoped he would do.

"Take your hands off my client! I said let him go! I would advise you to calm down or you will be facing an assault charge, Mr. Mayhem!" Solomon threatened him.

He paid Solomon no mind while he continued to choke Geno. In the midst of their physically struggle, Mayhem and Solomon's eyes locked into one another. In that brief moment, Mayhem came to his senses. He released his death grip from around Geno's throat. Geno played up the incident. When Mayhem released him, he thrust himself back in his chair violently. He wore the look of a man afraid for his life even though he really wasn't. He pretended to be gasping for air. He took his hand and rubbed his throat as if he needed to soothe away his pain.

"Can I have some water please? My throat is very dry," Geno requested rather calmly for a man who was just seconds away from being choked to death. Sensing he needed a break to compose himself, Mayhem walked out of the room to get Geno some water. Detective Swanson, the lead detective assigned to the case approached him in the hallway to discuss what just transpired in the interrogation room. Mayhem merely brushed him off and paid his attempt to reprimand him about his physically assaulting Geno no mind. In fact, Mayhem threatened to go to Swanson's superior officer and have him removed from the case if he attempted to interfere with his questioning Geno any further. Swanson backed down because he realized he was just a small player in a case that had multiple layers to it.

"Geno, are you okay?" Solomon asked.

"I'm fine, kid. Mayhem is playing right into my hands. Just sit back and watch me work," he uttered to him in a very low tone. Seconds later, Mayhem returned to room with a cup of water for Geno. He forcefully placed the cup down in front of Geno, who retrieved it and sip slowly from it while he listened to Mayhem speak.

"So, what's it gonna be Geno?" Mayhem asked bluntly. He appeared to be at his wits end. Their mental game of war over the years had pushed him to the brink of total frustration at this point.

"How about you cut that camera off so we can have a very frank off the record conversation? I may have a few things to say about this case which could prove to be beneficial," Geno offered.

Mayhem contemplated his request for a second. He knew he had no chance of breaking Geno down to get a confession out of him because Geno was as rock solid as they came. He had no evidence to tie Geno to the murders at all. He had run out of options at this point and was desperate. He turned around and glanced in the direction of the two way mirror that allowed for Swanson to review his interrogation from the other room. He instructed him to turn off the cameras and he reluctantly complied.

"I'm all ears," Mayhem stated humbly.

"Now, Mayhem, you and I both knew you are at a crossroads with this case you have against me. Without Sam to testify, your entire case is up shit's creek. You have no way to tie me to those bank accounts. All you have is a gang of money seized, but no one to connect it to as being the source. You can foolish try to pursue this case against me, but I think you know it's a losing cause. I'm sure your superiors are about to have your head on a platter soon for botching what you presented as a slam dunk case against me. With all of those dead bodies and no concrete evidence to connect me or anyone else to them, I think we both can agree that Solomon here will have a field day in court tearing both cases to shreds easily by creating a reasonable doubt. We can add in the fact I know you paid Judge Artest off to try and deny me bail. You don't have to admit it because I can tell it's true by your facial expression right now. It won't take much for a man with my vast amount of resources to apply pressure to get him to admit as much to save his own ass. It would be a shame for you to be brought before the Bar association for that kind of allegation wouldn't it? Despite our differences, I would hate to see you lose your career and everything you worked so hard for over this one case. Being honest with you, I have a lot of respect for you as a man and an attorney. You may not believe me, but it's the truth. You may not agree with how I conduct my business and that's fine. However, I think it's time we end this thing between us. Let's say we come to an agreement that is mutually beneficial to the both of us," Geno suggested.

Mayhem was clearly between a rock and a hard place. Everything Geno just spoke was the unmitigated truth. He knew he took a risk to bribe Judge Artest and it could possibly come back to bite him in the ass if Geno forced the issue. Truthfully speaking, Artest had no loyalty to anyone but himself. He would definitely rat Mayhem out if it meant saving his own neck. He couldn't imagine the shame he would bring down upon Olivia and his family name if his actions became public. Despite his immense dislike for Geno, at this point he was open to any bone that was thrown his way. Geno's words of praise surprised him. They appeared to be sincere, but with Geno, one could never be sure.

"What do you propose?" he asked.

"I have a way you can come out of this looking like a hero in exchange for you dropping these ridiculous charges against me. Let's make a deal," Geno proposed. He knew his offer was a crapshoot because Mayhem had always been a by the book type of man, but it was worth a shot. He had nothing to lose at this point.

"I'm all ears," Mayhem reluctantly stated.

Geno laid out his proposition thoroughly. Mayhem listened attentively to every word he spoke. He had to admit Geno's plan was a win win situation for the both of them. It would take some skillful maneuvering on his part to pull it off, but it was his only hope to come out of this situation with his dignity intact and his job secure. He would have to let Geno walk, but he could live with that despite his personal disdain for him. The two men shook hands and agreed to put their differences aside. Young Solomon was just a fly on the wall for some of the most brilliant and effective legal maneuvering he could ever hope to witness. If all things went as planned, Geno would soon be a free man and Mayhem would be able to save face and keep his job. All they could hope for was no snags to come along to thwart the plan.

Chapter 22

For the first time in his life, Gavin Mayhem was nervous speaking in the public. It was a strange feeling for a man who had litigated hundreds of legal cases over the years, but today was different. He called a press conference to address Geno's case as well as the murders of Sam Bradford and the federal agents who were charged with protecting him. He had to choose his words carefully because what he said could make or break his career. When he stepped up to the podium, the first thing he noticed was the packed room of reporters in front of him. He knew they planned to bombard him with questions after he gave his speech, but it was his intention to read his prepared statement and to keep the Q&A session to a minimum. Once he composed himself and shook off his jitters, Mayhem readied himself to address the crowd.

"I called you all here today to address the Geno Caprese case as well as the tragic deaths of Sam Bradford and several federal agents. My sincerest condolences go out to the family members of all those affected by this horrendous crime. After careful consideration and several new developments, we have decided to drop all charges against Geno Caprese due to their being insufficient evidence to proceed with the case against him. We would like to also issue a public apology to Mr. Caprese and his family for the undue duress that this case has placed upon them. With respect to the murders of the six federal agents and federal witness, Sam Bradford, we have received credible information to conclude that these atrocious crimes were sanctioned by a high ranking member of the Lopez Cartel, who is based in Sinaloa, Mexico. They happen to be one of the largest importers of cocaine into the United States. Specifically, Mr. Manuel Lopez, one of the leaders of this Sinaloan cartel, is our prime suspect in the case. Mr. Bradford was working with us on a separate case involving Mr. Lopez. We now believe that the false information Mr. Bradford gave us in reference to Mr. Caprese was an attempt on his part to gain leniency in his own legal

*situation. I would also like to state that Mr.
Manuel Lopez is now in federal custody and
will be made to stand trial for these
horrendous crimes. We intend to make an
example out of Mr. Lopez. We want to send
a message today that the United States
government will not tolerate the violence
from these Mexican drug cartels spoiling over
across the border placing the lives of
American citizens in jeopardy. These criminals
who commit these violent crimes will be
arrested and held accountable for their
actions. At this time, I would like to open the
floor for a brief round of questions from the
press."*

Mayhem answered the questions posed by the
press with short, direct responses. He didn't want to
feed them more information than was necessary.
The more questions he answered, the more likely it
was they would have a chance to poke holes in the
cleverly weaved spin on this matter that Geno had
concocted and he executed. After his press
conference, Mayhem got to work on preparing his
case against Manuel Lopez. Once he secured a
conviction against him, his plan was to work with
the DEA to go after the entire Lopez Cartel. That
wasn't part of his original agreement with Geno, but
he figured he might as well take advantage of the
situation and fully work it to his advantage.

Mayhem was now viewed even more so as a man who stood for justice and who was fearless in going after major crime figures as opposed to foot soldiers. He was bombarded with requests to appear on television shows and to do interviews with major magazines. He received a level of adulation and praise which he had never received in his entire career. He was no longer a locally recognized figure, but this case put him before a national audience. Though he hated to admit it, he owed it all to Geno.

With Manuel Lopez in custody, Mayhem had the perfect suspect to convict of these crimes. As it turned out, when he was originally arrested, Geno was visited in prison by an inmate named, Pepe Soto, a high ranking member of the Lopez family's organization within the prison system. Pepe informed Geno that Manuel had become a costly liability to the organization. A good majority of the murders that took place as a result of the feud between the Lopez and Nunez Cartels were sanctioned by Manuel against his brother's wishes. The brutal murders drew too much attention from local law enforcement and proved to be bad for business.

While his brothers worked diligently to broker a peace treaty with the leadership of the Nunez Cartel so that both organizations could continue to conduct profitable business, Manuel was a loose cannon who went behind his brother's backs and continued to order executions of members of the Nunez family. He didn't want peace with them. He wanted to totally eliminate the competition so that the Lopez Cartel was the sole source of cocaine in Sinaloa. It was also discovered that Manuel was doing side deals with other drug families outside of Sinaloa without their knowledge. His disloyalty to the family made him expendable to his brothers.

When he was indicted along with Peter and Sam Bradford for money laundering, that was the straw that broke the camel's back. Not only did they have to deal with the law in Mexico, they would now have more heat on them from the United States government because of his reckless actions. Once the U.S. government had him on their radar, it was only a matter of time before they turned their attention toward the entire organization.

The other Lopez brothers agreed amongst themselves that they had worked too hard and made too many sacrifices to build up their business to the level it had achieved for it to be destroyed by one wayward brother who acted out of pure selfish agreed. Consequently, they voted against killing him, but decided that a long prison sentence was the best way to minimize the damage he could do to the family business. When they found out about Geno's arrest and how it was connected with their brother's case, they came up with a plan that proved to be mutually beneficial to them and Geno as well. The Lopez brothers were extremely wealthy and used their wealth to pay off countless American government officials to be able to continue to import tons of cocaine into the country for so long. Their government connections allowed them access to information such as the location of federal witnesses in protective custody. They got Pepe to give Geno information on Sam Bradford's location so he could be killed before he had a chance to testify against him. In exchange, they wanted Geno to pin Sam's murder on Manuel. They wanted it to look like retaliation for Sam intending to testify against Manuel in his case.

Pepe also gave Geno information as to where Manuel was hiding out after his federal indictment on the money laundering charges. When he made his deal with Mayhem, Geno informed him that Manuel was hiding out in Atlanta, Georgia, under an alias name. That was how they were able to apprehend him so easily. Peter was left alive because his testimony was needed to convict Manuel for the money laundering charges. He would definitely get life in prison at the very least for the murders and the money laundering charges would be the final nail in his coffin. He would never see the light of day on the streets again. That was the steep price he had to pay for betraying his crime family. To seal his fate, Geno made sure the murder scene resembled the style of killings Manuel ordered back in Mexico. That was why he wanted Sam's throat slit so viciously. He wanted it to resemble a Mexican bowtie, which was something Manuel was famous for ordering his assassins to do, particular to police officers, to send a very clear message.

Although it was an intricate and complex plan, the end result worked out perfectly for everybody involved. With Manuel no longer around to spill more blood on the streets of Sinaloa, The Lopez brothers were able to work toward forming a mutually beneficial working relationship with the Nunez brothers so they could both continue to make massive amounts of money and end the violence between them. Because of his efforts, Geno now had a powerful Mexican ally in the Lopez brothers at his disposal. He was also a free man again. He no longer had any legal entanglements to hinder his actions. He could now get back to his normal life and resume the seat at the helm of his empire.

Geno's first order of business was to decide how he planned to deal with the issues which were presented to him by Jericho and Jia about his top underboss, Sal. Because of his love for Sal, he put the issue on the back burner for a minute before he approached him. He needed to know where they really stood with one another before he decided how to handle his behavior. He couldn't let the disrespect Sal showed Jia stand without any repercussions. He had to be held accountable for his actions. He also wouldn't tolerate his efforts to try and fill his shoes as the boss. He learned that lesson from his issues with his own envious brother, Silvio. He would never make that mistake again.

Chapter 23

Being incarcerated, albeit for a brief spell, gave Geno a chance to really appreciate his freedom. He got a chance to see life from another perspective. He was given a front row seat to see how life was like for the poor and downtrodden clients he represented who were recycled through the criminal justice system repeatedly. The living conditions of daily life in jail were unfit for any man to have to endure. From the poor quality of the food to the mice and rats that ran about his jail cell as though they were inmates being housed as well, Geno got enough of a visual of prison life to know he wanted no parts of it again in his lifetime. He truly valued his freedom now more than ever. He worked out a deal with Mayhem whereby he agreed to give him a heads up if any information came across his desk involving either him or the Caprese Foundation. Despite their rocky history, Geno believed he could trust Mayhem to keep his word. He had just as much to lose as Geno did. Like it or not, they were bonded by the secret deal they brokered together.

Geno's prison experience also forced a significant change in his approach to business moving forward. He decided he could no longer live in two worlds by funding his legal business entities with illegal proceeds. It left him open to experience situations like he just endured. He decided it was time for him to sever all ties with any illicit revenue streams and dedicate his full focus on his many legitimate business entities. He knew some of his inner circle wouldn't be happy with his decision, but his mind was made up. He had to make the best choice for himself and his family. Being away from them for that brief spell further reinforced how important they were to him. With all of the disloyalty he had encountered recently, one thing he knew for sure was Carina and his children would never betray him. He would bet his entire fortune on that fact.

Geno was also motivated to do more to help out inmates who came home from jail and had a difficult time getting back on their feet. His talks on the yard with young men like Remy educated him about the struggles they faced in society being convicted felons. Outside of the monetary contributions he already made to several non-profit organizations that focused their efforts on this population, he knew there was much more he could do. He could easily use his power and influence in the business community to encourage some of his fellow business owners to provide more entry level jobs for these individuals. He also intended to meet with the heads of several local universities that he played golf with on occasion to develop scholarship funds specifically for convicted felons to assist them with paying college tuition. He had even more innovative ideas flowing through his brain which he intended to work on implementing. The money the government seized from Sam Bradford's bank was just a small portion of his finances. Geno wasn't foolish enough to allow just Sam to handle all of his money. He had other bankers he used to hide even larger pots of his cash. He had more than enough money to live lavishly off of for the rest of his life so it was nothing for him to share it with the less fortunate.

Now that he was free of all legal restraints, it was time for him to get back down to business at the Foundation. He planned to meet with all of the members of the board individually to feel them out and to get a sense of their level of loyalty to the Foundation. If he didn't get the kind of positive vibe he was looking for from any of them, he planned to give the green light to Jericho to snuff out their existence without a second thought. After his experience with Sam, he couldn't afford to have another snitch in his camp. He knew it was only so many times a man could cheat the system like he just did without getting pinched.

Geno also needed to deal with the Sal situation as soon as possible. He had yet to confront him about his sexually accosting Jia as well as the things Jericho and Cesare brought to his attention. Up to this point, he acted as though everything was fine between them when he interacted with Sal at the office. Geno was disturbed and genuinely disappointed by Sal's behavior. He expected much better from him given their history together. He had to put the love he had for Sal to the side and face the reality he wasn't the same person he used to be. Having a taste of power corrupted the bond between them.

Before he dealt with Sal, Geno needed to check on Milton Jackson. Cesare told him about his recent drinking problem and Geno needed to see what, if anything, he could do to help his comrade. He was sympathetic to his struggle with coming to grips with his brother's death. To hear that Milton had fallen apart and began to lean on alcohol as his crutch greatly disturbed Geno. He couldn't stand by and lose another strong soldier without making an effort to try and be there for him. That was why he and Jericho were headed to his house now. He needed to see for himself how badly his good friend had fallen off. He planned to do an intervention to try and get him the help he needed to return back to his old self, if that were at all possible.

"How does it feel to be a free man, Geno?" Jericho asked.

"It feels good, brother. Now that I'm home, I'm gonna make some major changes in my life and at the Foundation. I want you and Cesare to be a big part of my future plans for this family. As of this moment, everything we do will be above board and legal. That means no more dirty money for us," Geno stated bluntly. He wanted to leave no room for his words to be misinterpreted.

"I'm all in. Just tell me what you need me to do," Jericho stated without hesitation.

"That's what I wanted to hear. I'm glad to see you're on board. How is Cesare doing since that thing went down?" he inquired.

"That's a whole other matter in itself. I think we've created a monster, but I have it under control. We can talk about that later," Jericho replied.

"Geno, we're here," Clay informed him as he pulled up into the driveway of Milton's home. He parked the Maybach next to Milton's burnt orange colored Lamborghini. The car was covered in dust and appeared as though it hadn't been driven in weeks. Geno got a bad feeling inside when he and Jericho stepped out of the car. He glanced around Milton's property and couldn't believe what saw.

The lawn looked like it hadn't been cut in weeks.
Milton's trash cans overflowed with trash so high
the lids wouldn't close. The pungent odor from
them made both Geno and Jericho covered their
noses. He could only imagine what the inside of the
house looked like.

While Clay waited for them in the car, Geno and
Jericho walked up to the front door and rung the
bell several times, but got no answer. They waited a
few minutes before they decided to walk around to
the rear of the house. When they peaked inside the
door to the patio area, they noticed the television
was on and they could see Milton slouched over on
the couch passed out. Jericho fidgeted with the
door and realized it was unlocked. He and Geno
decided to let themselves in.

The sound of the door opening awoke Milton
out of his deep slumber. He almost tripped over his
own feet when he tried to stand up. Milton was
dressed in a pair of gym shorts and a wife beater t-
shirt. His rough physical appearance and the strong
stench of alcohol in the room were clear indicators
he was intoxicated. There were funky sweat socks
and filthy boxer shorts sprawled across the floor.
The entire house looked a mess. Geno couldn't
believe his eyes. The man in front of him couldn't
possibly be the same Milton Jackson he knew. His
body had to have been invaded by an
extraterrestrial alcoholic. He shook his head in

disbelief as he made his way into the house. He was stopped in his tracks when he saw Milton had a gun in his hand pointed at him.

"Milton, what the hell is going on with you, brother?" Geno asked him. He had his hands raised in the air in a non-threatening position.

"Don't come any closer. You can stay right where you are. I'm minding my own business. I didn't invite you into my house. What are you doing here? You don't care about me. You only care about your damn self," he shouted at him angrily.

Milton took his free hand and swiped sweat from his brow. That split second was just enough time for Jericho to be able to reach for his 9mm Glock. He had it aimed center mass at Milton ready to end his existence with a single shot. He was about to squeeze the trigger, but Geno motioned for him to stand down.

"Calm down, Milton. It's me, Geno. Put that thing away. We come in peace, brother. Let's talk like gentleman," Geno tried to reason with him. He knew it was the alcohol and not Milton in control right now. The scene in the room was tense. Both Milton and Jericho still had their weapons drawn. Neither one of them looked ready to budge an inch.

"I ain't scared of you, Caprese. You think the world revolves around you, but it doesn't. Other people's lives matter too. My brother's life mattered, but you didn't give a damn about him dying. He's dead because of you. I lost my brother because of your shit. Why couldn't you die instead of him? Why do you always have to be the one who gets away scot free? It ain't fair! It just ain't fair!" he yelled.

"Just give me the word and I'll take the shot, Geno," Jericho interjected. He had no problem filling Milton up with hot lead if it were necessary.

"Let's get it on, motherfucker!" Milton shot back waving his gun recklessly in the air. Geno stood square in the middle of both them. He was the only thing standing between Milton's house turning into a murder scene.

"Nobody's killing anybody today! I need both of you to put those guns down now. We're all family in here. Milton, I love you like a brother and I loved Jarvis the same way. Deep down inside you know I would take a bullet for you if necessary. You know it's true. I know it's not you talking now. It's the alcohol doing the talking. Put that gun down and let's talk like men!" Geno demanded.

Before Milton had a chance to respond, Geno darted toward him and tackled him down to the ground. In his inebriated stated, his reflexes were slow. Milton was physically no match for Geno. They wrestled on the ground briefly before Milton's gun fell out of his hand. Jericho raced over to where it was located and picked it up. Geno was able to overpower Milton and had him pinned down on the ground. Milton continued to fight back as best as he could, but Geno's brute strength eventually forced him to surrender.

"Go ahead and kill me. Get it over with now! I'm ready to die!" Milton yelled in a manic state. Tears streamed down his cheeks. Since he was no longer a threat, Geno got up from on top of him and sat down on the couch. Jericho remained in position ready to shoot. He could easily get off a lethal shot before Milton had a chance to blink. He waited for Geno to give him the word.

"I'm not going to kill you, Milton. You're my brother. We're going to get you the help you need to get back on your feet. What would Jarvis say if he saw you like this? He would tell you to get your shit together and you know I'm right," Geno stated sternly like a father scolding his wayward child. He hoped he got through to him so he could halt this train wreck that had become his life.

Milton couldn't say a word. He just balled up like a baby and cried uncontrollably. Geno wrapped his arms around him to hug him like a big brother should do. He sympathized with his pain. He hated seeing his good friend in such a disheveled state. If it were anyone else who pointed a gun at him, he would've given the order for Jericho to kill that person without hesitation, but Milton was family. He had to spare his life. He valued soldiers like him more than money. In his right state of mind, Milton was a tried and true warrior. He deserved at least one chance to redeem himself.

"I need help, Geno. I need help! I'm sorry, man. I don't know what I was thinking," Milton stated regretful for his actions. He knew he was messed up mentally, emotionally, and physically. He let alcohol become his best friend and it was about to destroy him slowly if he didn't get help.

"It's all good, brother. Besides, you and I both know that I've stared down bigger guns than that little pea shooter you had pointed at me," Geno joked in an attempt to lighten the mood in the room. Milton cracked a smile and laughed. In that brief moment, Geno saw a brief glimpse of his old friend come to the surface. The real Milton Jackson was a good dude. Geno would do whatever was necessary to help him get his mind right. The first step he had to make was to deal with his drinking problem. In his right mind, Geno would trust Milton with his life. That meant a lot to him with all of the betrayal he experienced lately. He needed solid men like him around for his future plans. Whatever it took, Geno would be right there with Milton on his road to recovery.

Chapter 24

Ever since Geno came back to the office full-time, Sal sensed something wasn't right between them. Their relationship wasn't as close as it used to be. Geno didn't say anything in particular that was confrontational or hostile toward him, but he knew Geno well enough to know when he was studying an individual to try and read their actions. He could tell he was under a microscope every time he was around Geno lately. Geno held secret meetings with the Board and some of his investors without including him. That was unlike Geno to do given the fact Sal was supposed to be his second in command. When he asked him about it, Geno simply said the meetings were nothing serious, but just discussions about new ideas he had. He told Sal he would bring him into the loop when the time was right. Sal knew that was nonsense and just an attempt on Geno's part to appease him and hide his true intentions.

Sal was sure both Cesare and Jericho had been in Geno's ear since he came home from jail bad mouthing him at every turn. He also noticed every time he saw Jia around the office recently she went out of her way to avoid him. He sensed she had said something to Geno about their little incident. Sal was well aware of how close she and Geno were and he partially regretted pushing up on her so aggressively, but it was too late to take his actions back. Besides, in his mind, she was just another fine piece of young ass he wanted to sex. He reasoned that if Geno let her come between them, then their friendship wasn't as tight as it should be. If Geno was pissed at him over Jia, he was in violation of the G code. Sal believed that made men should never fall out over a woman under any circumstances. It went against man law in every way.

Sal had been around Geno long enough to know how he thought almost as well as Geno knew himself. For example, Sal picked up over the years Geno's tendency to study a person thoroughly to try and find a weakness he could use to his advantage to control the interaction between them. He also became guarded in his interaction with someone right before he planned to spring into action with one of his diabolical mind games he liked to play with people. Sal saw the handwriting was on the wall. His gut told him Geno had something in the works for him, but he wasn't one to back down from a confrontation. He was just as much of a gangster as Geno was. Geno knew this about him very well which was why he was being cautious and calculative before he approached him. Sal was prepared for whatever Geno brought his way.

All of these tell tale signs were clear indicators for Sal that his desire to branch off and do his own thing was the best move for him to make at this time. He felt he had learned enough from Geno over the years to be able to run his own corporation just as competently as Geno, albeit on a smaller scale at this time. He had no problem starting out small to get his feet wet. That was why he was on his way to Los Angeles currently to a meeting his attorney, Blair Simmons, setup for him with another group of his clients, Gaku and Akito Hashimoto. The Hashimoto brothers were two young, wealthy Japanese entrepreneurs who were interested in breaking into the video gaming industry. Their company, Hashimoto Electronics, was a small, Japanese company that was financially struggling at the moment. They had an inexpensive line of high definition televisions on the market currently that did pretty well. They were looking to expand their brand and product line in an effort to get out of debt. When Blair presented them Sal's proposal for his video gaming company, they were excited and wanted in.

Sal had several million dollars of his own to invest in the company, but the first thing he learned from Geno was it was always wise to use other people's money first in business. While he was working at the Foundation, Sal picked Jeremy's brain every chance he could to get some insider tips on the gaming industry to help him get the upper hand on the competition. Jeremy had no clue he was being used in Sal's grand scheme that didn't include CITD, but he would find out soon enough once his company was up and running. Sal was excited about the prospect of this joint venture being a massive success. He knew it would take a good minute to get off the ground, but he was patient enough to see his idea through to the end.

This was Sal's fifth trip out to Los Angeles and he fell more in love with the place every time he visited. Before he hopped on his flight, he left Geno a voicemail message that stated he was taking a few days off to relax, but he didn't tell him where he was going specifically. He sipped on a glass of bourbon while he waited for his flight to land. He had been on the plane for over five hours already. Even though he was in first class, he was getting restless. The flight attendant stated over the intercom system that the flight would be landing in less than thirty minutes. Her announcement was music to his ears. He couldn't wait to touch down in Los Angeles to soak up some sunshine. Some eighty degree weather was a welcome change from the cold fall weather on the East Coast. He needed a change of scenery and the land of pretty women in bikinis was the perfect place for him to start anew. While he contemplated his new future, he snapped out of his daydream when the plane jerked violently and he felt the effect of the wheels scraping against the ground. He was relieved his plane had finally landed.

When the plane was finished taxing to the gate, Sal quickly unfastened his seatbelt. The flight attendant gave the go ahead for passengers to exit the plane and Sal was the first person out of his seat. He quickly grabbed his luggage from the overhead storage compartment and raced off the plane. His attorney had a car service waiting for him to take him to his meeting. Once he took care of business, he figured it was only right he took time out to enjoy the beach and the pretty girls who were there to work on their tans. After all, he was a single man with a healthy libido. Sal felt he deserved to enjoy himself.

He quickly made his way through LAX to the ground transportation area. He located the limousine driver that was there for him and hopped inside of the limo. He was on his way to the beginning stages of his new life. He had already purchased himself a condominium on the beach where he planned to live. He also rented out a plush office for his new business venture. There was no turning back for him at this point. He had no regrets about his decision to part ways with the Foundation without saying a word. If Geno had an issue with his leaving, then that was his problem. He didn't feel as though he owed him a thing. He hoped Geno and the Caprese Foundation were a part of his past. He told himself this was the good life he was meant to enjoy. Sal lit up a cigar, poured himself a glass of champagne, and rolled down the window to enjoy the California sunshine.

Chapter 25

While he listened to Sal's voicemail message about him going on vacation, Geno was amused Sal thought he was about to get one up on him without his knowledge. He should have known better than to think Geno could ever be anyone's fool. He knew damn well Sal was blowing smoke up his ass. He wasn't just going on vacation, but he had something else up his sleeve. After his conversations with Jericho and Cesare about Sal and his attempts to flex on them at the office, he wanted to find out just what Sal was up to for sure so he would best know how to deal with him. That was why he got John Lucci to put a tail on him to monitor his every move. Thanks to Lucci, Geno knew all about Sal's other trips to Los Angeles prior to this one, but never said a word to him. He just let him play his hand out before he decided to show his.

John Lucci came through for him like he always did. Geno found out all about the large sums of money Sal recently transferred to various banks in Los Angeles. He discovered he had put his house on the market for sale. He got Geno a heap of background information on Sal's attorney, Blair Simmons. He observed all of his lunch and dinner meetings with the Hashimoto brothers. With all of this useful information at his disposal, it was clear to Geno that Sal had something major up his sleeve that he had no intention of involving him in. Geno had to face the fact that Sal was not his brother, but another person who turned his back on him despite all of the things he did for him.

Geno felt it was his business acumen that made Sal a rich man legitimately when he could have just left him out in the cold to earn on his own out in the streets breaking law. By exposing him to the spoils of corporate America, Geno thought he had created a lifelong ally and business partner. Instead, for whatever reason, Sal chose to become his competition. That was a foolish move on his part because wise businessmen like Geno never revealed all of their tricks of the trade to anyone. Geno planned to give Sal a lesson he would never forget. He planned to have the last laugh at his old friend's expense very soon.

Despite his feelings of disappointment with Sal, Geno refused to let him dampen his mood. To celebrate his freedom, Geno decided to have a big dinner party at Maggie's tonight. He closed down the restaurant to the public because he wanted it to just be a family affair. He felt the need to be surrounded by his closest loved ones to regain his mental focus after all of the betrayal and backstabbing he experienced lately. When he glanced around the room, he was glad to see Carina and his children seated near him. His mother even decided to come to the party. Geno hadn't seen her much since she decided to sell her home after Leonardo died. She moved into a ritzy, senior residential facility and maintained an active social life despite her advanced age. She even had a new love interest in her life to keep her company. Geno didn't mind because if she was happy, then so was he.

Jericho and Nina were there as well. Nina's belly had doubled in size. She looked like she was about to give birth to twins. Shavon decided to fly in from Connecticut for the party. Cesare arrived late with Sheila, his newest love interest. Milton Jackson was in attendance. He had completed an inpatient detoxification program for his drinking problem and appeared to be back on track. Geno was glad to see him back in good spirits. Geno also decided to invite Jia and Solomon, as well as Jeremy. He considered them to be members of his extended family. It was only right they joined in on the festivities.

"Man, this food is good! Give my compliments to the chef!" Jericho declared as he finished up his second plate of lasagna.

"Hey, we Italians know how to throw down in the kitchen too, brother. It's about time you got in touch with your Sicilian roots," Geno teased him. Jericho laughed while he continued to stuff his face.

The chefs at the restaurant prepared a massive food spread that included not only Italian dishes, but they made a wide variety of ethnic food selections for everyone to enjoy. The food was delicious judging by the way everyone went back for second and third plates. All of the adults sipped from the finest house wines while Gianna and Stefan drank juice. Geno had the DJ from the lounge to play a wide range of musical selections that everyone could enjoy. When she was done eating, Carina pulled Geno out on the dance floor to show off his dance moves. Not one to disappoint a crowd, Geno and Carina entertained everybody with their attempts to do the latest dances. Gianna and Stefan cracked up laughing at their parents efforts to try and be hip. Everybody got up on the dance floor and joined them. Jericho even let loose and danced with Nina briefly. Geno's dinner party turned into an all out stone cold groove thing.

Geno wore himself out on the dance floor. While everybody continued to enjoy the party, he decided to take a break to rest his tired feet. Cesare saw him seated by himself and decided to join him. Shortly thereafter, Jericho joined them. It was a sight to behold to see the three patriarchs of the Caprese family together. Leonardo Caprese had to be looking down from heaven proud to see his sons have such a close relationship. It was what he always wanted even though he was unable to make it happen before he passed away. The three of them had a good time talking about a wide array of things while everybody else continued to party.

"So, Geno, what are you going to do about Sal? I wanna know what our next move is," Jericho stated abruptly out of the blue. Cesare's ears perked as he awaited Geno's response.

"Yeah, Geno, what are we going to do about him?" Cesare chimed in. Ever since the hit they carried out on Sam and the federal agents, he was itching to get in on some more action.

"Fellas, don't worry about Sal. I have something in store for him. He won't even see it coming. I don't want to talk about him anymore. This night is about us, the Caprese family. I wanna talk about my little nephew that's on the way. When is he due to make his appearance in the world?"

"He'll be here in another three months," Jericho replied. He couldn't wait to meet his son either. He understood Geno's desire to have some fun after his ordeal, but he was eager to get a piece of Sal. He didn't understand Geno's nonchalant attitude about him, but he had to accept it for right now.

"Let's toast to the next generation. He's the future," Geno proclaimed. After polishing off two bottles of wine already, it was safe to say Geno was drunk. He earned the right to unwind and have fun. He ordered another round of drinks for him and his brothers. He knew he would have a massive hangover in the morning, but he didn't care. He was out with family and, at the moment, that was all that counted.

Chapter 26

Sal was in heaven right now as he sat up in his bed. He felt a little groggy, but it was all good. He rolled over to his right side to see a beautiful twenty something year old, thickly built brunette with perfectly shaped 36DD sized breasts laying next to him. When he glanced over to his left side, there was a beautiful blonde with the perfect little ass sound asleep. He couldn't recall either of their names. After drinking multiple bottles of champagne and inhaling countless lines of cocaine the night before, he couldn't remember a thing about what went down. However, judging by the way their clothes were scattered all around his bedroom, they had to have had a damn good time.

He carefully got up out of the bed so he wouldn't wake up his guests. He made his way to the bathroom to relieve himself. He reached into his medicine cabinet to retrieve some aspirin to try and get rid of his massive headache. He hopped into the shower in hopes that once the hot water hit him it would help him sober up. He had a big meeting today and was already behind schedule. It was eleven o'clock in the morning and his meeting was at noon. He needed to get ready in a hurry if he wanted to make it on time.

Once he was done in the shower, he grabbed a towel, wrapped it around him, and returned to his bedroom. His two guests were still fast asleep. He pulled back the covers to get one last glance at their beautiful bodies before he woke them up. They both were positioned on their stomachs and he was able to get a good view of their backsides. He was in a trance for a moment as he enjoyed the view, but then he reminded himself it was time for him to regain his focus. He had fun the night before, but it was time for them to go. They had served their purpose and he no longer needed them around.

Since he moved out to Los Angeles, Sal's condo had been a revolving door of beautiful women coming and going. He wasn't looking for a relationship with any of them. He just wanted to have a good time with no strings attached. He had no time for love in his life. He was too focused on making money. He bent down and smacked both women on their backside to roust them out of their deep sleep. They both jumped up instantly.

"Hey, Daddy, I like it a little rough. Are you ready for another round?" the blonde asked. She rolled over and spread her legs wide apart so Sal could get a good view of her private parts. She reached over to stroke the brunette's hair gently. The brunette, in turn, rolled over and planted a light kiss on the blonde's erect nipple. Sal was tempted to hop back in the bed with them and continue their party from the night before, but he reminded himself he had more important things to do today.

"I would love to doll face, but I got things to do. You two need to get dressed and get out of here. I can call you an Uber driver if you need a ride home," he stated rather rudely.

"So, we fucked your brains out last night and now you're kicking us out? Damn, Sal, is that how it is?" the brunette asked. Her mood changed quickly. She went from being turned on to being pissed off by Sal's comment.

"That's exactly how it is, ladies. Get your shit and get up out of here!" he said with a more forceful tone. The look on his face let them know this wasn't a game. Sal was a dangerous man. Things could get ugly if they didn't do as he said. They both jumped out of the bed and grabbed their clothes, which were scattered all around the room. They got dressed quickly. The blonde flashed Sal the middle finger on her way out of the door.

They didn't even wait for him to call them a ride. Sal didn't mind one bit. He was glad to be rid of them. Once he was sure the coast was clear, he went back into his bedroom to find something to throw on.

Sal's move to California was the best thing he had ever done in his life. He didn't miss a thing about Baltimore, Maryland or the East Coast at all. They could keep those frigid cold winters and snowfall. He preferred the beautiful sunshine and beaches of the West Coast. Once he was fully dressed, he grabbed the keys to his Ferrari and headed out the door. He hopped on the elevator and headed down to the garage. He had a ten minute ride to his office. Today was the day his life would change forever. He planned to finally sign the paperwork to make his deal with the Hashimoto brothers official. When he made it to his office building and into his suite, he was happy to see Blair and the Hashimoto brothers were already there. His secretary, Margaret, supplied them with coffee and donuts and entertained them until he arrived.

"Gentleman, I'm sorry I'm a little late. I hope you don't hold it against me and decide not to cut that big check today," Sal joked.

"It's no problem at all, Sal. We do business a little difference over here on the West Coast. We're not sticklers for little details like punctuality over

here. We just want to close the deals," Blair replied.
The Hashimoto brothers nodded in agreement.
They all shook hands and headed into his office to
conduct business. They all took a seat around the
conference table in Sal's office. Blair reached into
his briefcase and pulled out a set of contracts. He
placed them on the table for Sal to review. He
glanced over them briefly and nodded his head as
he read through some of the language it contained.

"Well, everything appears to be in order. Where
do I sign?" he asked.

"If you don't have any questions, you can sign
right here," Blair replied.

He had placed markers everywhere throughout
the contracts where everybody had to sign and
initial. It took a few minutes for them all to sign
and initial in the appropriate places. Once they were
all done, Blair handed Sal a check for twenty million
dollars. He glanced at the check and was
mesmerized. This was the first installment payment
of the Hashimoto's brothers investment in his
company. It was official. His company, Sal Bianchi
Incorporated, was now open for business. He
planned to take the gaming industry by storm. He
planned to show Geno he could be just as
successful as he was.

"Now that we have all of the formalities out of
the way, let's go celebrate the future. Lunch is on
me," Sal suggested.

"Where do you suggest we go?" Gaku Hashimoto asked.

"There's an awesome Hibachi restaurant right around the corner from here. We can walk there if you want," Sal replied.

"Let's go," Akito Hashimoto replied.

As they made their way out of his office headed out to eat lunch, Sal overheard Margaret engaged in a conversation with several men who spoke in a very loud tone. He excused himself to see what the commotion was. When he reached the lobby, he was surprised to see who it was. The last person he expected to see was Geno. He was accompanied by Jericho and Cesare. He didn't know what to do or say. He was at a loss for words. He had a stunned look on his face like he saw a ghost.

"Hey, there he is, my good friend Sal. I was just telling your wonderful secretary how long we've been friends. Tell her Sal," Geno uttered. He walked over and hugged Sal, but he pushed him away.

"Geno, what the hell are you doing here? Is this some kind of joke?" Sal uttered.

"Is this a joke? What do you mean? We're family Sal and I'm happy to see you as well as my business partners here," Geno replied. He walked over to shake hands with the Hashimoto brothers and Blair.

"What are you talking about?" Sal inquired.

"Oh, they didn't tell you I bought a controlling interest in their company a few weeks ago. It looks like we're going to be business partners again, Sal," Geno replied.

"Is this some kind of sick joke? Blair what the hell is going on?"

"It's true, Sal. Mr. Caprese is going to be in business with us. Is there a problem here?" he asked. He had no clue about the history between Geno and Sal. When Geno approached him about doing business with the Hashimoto brothers, he just took it as another major business deal he could close. His clients needed the money that Geno put on the table and they accepted his offer. They all had no idea they were being used as a pawn in one of Geno's twisted mind games. Sal didn't say a word. He looked in Blair's direction and then at Geno. Enraged, he rushed at Geno and tackled him to the ground.

"You greedy son of a bitch, you just couldn't stand to see me do my own thing, could you? You just have to be in control of everything!" Sal blurted out as he and Geno tussled. Jericho and Cesare pulled him off of Geno and pinned him up against the wall. He tried to break free, but was unsuccessful. Geno rose to his feet and walked in his direction.

"Sal, just so you know that check you have right there is my money. You work for me still. You didn't think you could outsmart me, did you? You thought you could set up shop out here and I wouldn't know about it? You thought you could take my ideas and use them to make yourself rich? Yes, Jeremy told me how you were always snooping around him asking questions about his business. Sal, no matter how hard you try, you can never be me. The way I see things, you have two options. You can either agree to work for me or you can walk away empty handed. Of course, there is always a third option, but let's not put that on the table just yet," Geno offered him. He glanced at Jericho to indicate that death was the last choice Sal had in this situation. Jericho would be happy to fulfill that contract. Sal had a choice to make and the clock was ticking.

"At this point, I have no choice, do I? You've got me by the balls," Sal stated reluctantly. His big plans just went up in smoke. In his mind, he cursed Geno out royally. He dared not speak ill of him to his face right now because he wasn't in a position of power at the moment.

"That's good news. I'm glad you made the right decision. Oh, and I'll be sending Solomon and Jia out here to oversee my interests. You will be reporting directly to them. Will that be a problem?" Geno asked.

"No, it won't be a problem," Sal replied humbly. His ego was just deflated like a hot air balloon.

"I'm glad to hear you are amenable to my terms. I must say it feels good to be able to expand the Caprese Foundation out to the West Coast. I'm all about growth and evolution. Also, it gives me a reason to bring Carina and the kids out here for vacation. Well, that concludes my business here. Gentleman, you enjoy the rest of your day," Geno stated rather calmly. He motioned for Jericho and Cesare to join him. The Caprese brothers exited Sal's office. They all shared a laugh at his expense. Sal was left behind to process the power play that just took place.

Chapter 27

"Jericho, wake up! It's time! Wake up, Jericho! We've gotta go now!" Nina yelled anxiously.

He heard her call his name, but it sounded like Nina was calling him from a far away distance. He was in a deep sleep; he thought she was part of one of his dreams. He realized it wasn't a dream when she slapped him forcefully in the face several times. The force of her blows woke him up in an instant. In a state of shock, as well as in pain, Jericho jumped up out of the bed cursing like a madman. He lost his balance and fell onto the floor landing on his backside.

"Woman, what the hell is wrong with you? Have you lost your mind hitting me like that? My ears are ringing," he hollered at her angrily. He struggled to get up on his feet.

"I'm sorry, baby. My water just broke. It's time! We've got to get to the hospital now!" she replied anxiously. She pulled back the covers so he could see the sheets were soaked with fluid. It took Jericho a minute to process what was going on and then it hit him. Their baby was on the way and they couldn't wait much longer to get to the hospital.

"Oh shit! Oh shit! This is real! Oh shit!" was all Jericho could say over and over. He was a bundle of nerves. He had anticipated the birth of his first child for months and now the moment for him to come into the world was here. He grabbed his pants off of the floor and threw on his sweater. He walked over to the other side of the bed to help Nina get to her feet.

"Go wake Shavon up. Go tell her she's about to be an Aunt. Call Geno and Cesare. Call everybody!" Nina ranted hysterically. She was so excited to finally meet her baby boy; she wanted the whole world to know he was on the way.

"Shavon, get up girl! We've gotta get to the hospital," Jericho yelled as he passed by her room.

He helped Nina make it to the stairs. She had her arm draped over his shoulder while they took their time and walked down the steps slowly. Shavon was home from school for the weekend. She came out of her room and saw them headed downstairs. She was dressed in her pajamas and bathrobe. She didn't care if anybody saw her dressed so crazily. She was about to become an aunt. She was beyond excited. She ran past them down the stairs.

"I'll start the truck while you help Nina get down the steps. My nephew is on his way! Auntie got you, baby!" she screamed full of joy.

By the time Jericho made it to the front door, she already had the truck started and the front passenger door open for Nina to get inside. Jericho was extra cautious as he helped Nina step up to get in the truck. Shavon hopped in the back seat while Jericho plopped himself behind the wheel. They raced at the speed of light en route to the hospital. Jericho sped through stop signs and traffic lights to get there. He didn't care if the police were out on the road. They would have to follow him to the hospital because there was no he was going to stop.

All Jericho cared about was getting to the hospital in time for his baby boy to come into the world healthy. That was all that mattered at the moment. When they reached the hospital, he hopped out of his truck and walked around to help Nina get out. Shavon ran inside of the hospital to get assistance. She came back out with a nurse and a wheel chair for Nina. She sat down in the chair and felt relieved to be off her feet. She was wheeled into the hospital and taken directly to a delivery room. Jericho didn't bother to park his truck. He left it right in the front area of the emergency room entrance and followed them inside. Shavon called Geno and Cesare to let them know what hospital they were at and instructed them to get there right away. They both arrived at the hospital within the hour. Carina stayed at home with the children.

After she was taken into the labor and delivery area, Nina was back there almost five hours before Jericho came out screaming at the top of his lungs. He yelled so loudly that his words were incoherent. He motioned for them all to come back to the delivery area. Jericho Malachi Jones had arrived in the world. He weighed nine pounds and six ounces. He was truly a sight to behold with his little chubby self. They all observed him while Jericho held him in his arms. Shavon never saw her brother so happy before. Nina was laid out in the hospital bed. She was exhausted from all of the pushing and shoving she had to do to force him out of her belly. Her precious baby boy was worth every bit of the pain she endured. Jericho handed little Jericho back to her so she could hold him.

"Look at my nephew. He looks just like you Jericho. That boy is going to be somebody special one day. I can see it already in his eyes," Geno stated proudly. He handed out cigars to Jericho and Cesare. They walked out of the room to go outside to have a smoke. They left Nina and Shavon alone to bond with little Jericho.

"Man, I can't believe this is real. I'ma father. I'm somebody's daddy," Jericho stated with tears in his eyes. He had never cried in public before, but he couldn't control himself. He didn't care who saw him.

"Cesare, you're up next, brother," Geno teased him.

"Nah, I'm not ready for that yet. I think I'll just enjoy being an Uncle again," Cesare stated honestly. He wasn't ready for that level of responsibility in his life right now. He had too many goals to achieve before he contemplated starting a family.

"You're in the big leagues now, Jericho. We've got another King to raise. Let's make him better and greater than all of us," Geno suggested.

Jericho nodded his head in agreement. He wanted his son to be better than him. He didn't want him to experience any of the harsh experiences he endured. With the help of his two brothers, he planned to keep him on the straight and narrow path. This was an epic Kodak moment to see the three Caprese men united together as a family. The birth of little Jericho was the perfect way to end off the drama filled year they all just had. He represented the possibility of a more fruitful and promising future for the family. They all took a big pull from their cigars and exhaled the smoke into the air as they pondered the possibilities.

The end

Notes

Notes (continued)

Other titles available by Thomas Long:

Dayvon's Story: A Thug's Life
Just Like Daddy
Money Kings: Just Like Daddy 2
Takeisha's Song: Cash Rules Everything
Unconventional Love
The Bodymore Homicide Novella series
Love TKO
High Society Gangster
High Society Gangster II

You can also find out additional information on Thomas Long at:

www.tlongwrites.com

http://www.tlongwrites.com/apps/blog

http://www.amazon.com/Thomas-Long/e/B0058OVYC6/

Facebook:

https://www.facebook.com/pages/Thomas-Long/169575816453538

Twitter and Instagram: @tlongmoney

Excerpt from the Bodymore Homicide Novella Series

"Jericho Jones: The Smooth Assassin"

Jericho was thirteen years old when his life was turned upside down. Up until that point, he lived as normal of a childhood as any other poor ghetto child in the inner city of Baltimore could, given his deprived social and financial circumstances. His family managed to survive with what little that they had. He lived in a run down, two bedroom house apartment with his mother, Raylene, and his little sister, Shavon, in northwest Baltimore City. He last saw his father when he was almost four years old. That was when he walked out on the family for no apparent reason, other than the fact that he was a deadbeat dad. All Jericho remembered about his father was that he was a tall slender, white man with a deep, bass filled voice. His mother told him that his name was Leonardo Caprese, and that he was a very bad person to her, but she never went into detail about what he did to her that was so bad. Truthfully, Jericho didn't care because when he saw how deeply his mother was hurt for years after he left them, he swore that he would protect her so that she could never feel that type of pain again. He also swore that if he ever ran across his father when he got older, he would make him pay for abandoning them.

Even though he was young, Jericho had an old soul and was very mature for his age. He took on the responsibility as the man of the house like a soldier. It was his job to make sure that Shavon got to school on time and ate properly, while Raylene worked long hours at Dandy's supermarket, which was located up the street from where they lived. She only made eight dollars per hour, but it was enough to pay their rent and to ensure that her children had food and clothing. They were a tight knit family unit with an unbreakable bond. Raylene made sure that she instilled good moral values into her children. Even though they were poor financially, she wanted them to be spiritually rich and to grow up to have upstanding character. They were all that each other had in this world and that was more than enough for the three of them. Money didn't matter because the love that they shared amongst them more than made up for their poor living condition. However, that all changed one fateful night.

On this very day ten years ago, Jericho and Shavon were fast asleep in their room when out of nowhere Jericho awoke to hear his mother as she loudly screamed out his name. He also smelled the scent of smoke. It had started to make its way into their room underneath of their closed bedroom door. When he got up and opened the bedroom door, he saw a large wall of flames headed towards him. He quickly closed the door behind him before he was engulfed in the flames. He could still hear his mother's screams from her bedroom, but he was unable to get to her. He felt helpless because he could do nothing to save her from such a horrible fate.

His brave nature made him want to go back out into the hallway and try to rescue his mother, but he knew that he had no chance of survival if he did. Instinctively, he woke Shavon up out of her sleep and carried her over to the bedroom window. She was startled by her brother's frantic state. With no time to explain, Jericho jumped out of the second story window first so that he could catch Shavon. Initially, she was afraid to jump until Jericho convinced her that she would be okay and that he would catch her when she landed. She built up the confidence to jump and she landed on top of him. They both tumbled to the ground awkwardly, but were out of harm's way of the fire. By this time, a swarm of fire trucks and police cars were also outside. Their neighbors were out in the street as well and watched the massive fire consume what used to be their home. Despite the firemen's efforts, Raylene sadly perished in the blaze. Jericho's last memory of his mother was the sound of her loud screams in obvious pain and agony. That sound still echoed in the back of his mind up until this day. He cried himself to sleep many nights and wished that it never happened, but it did. He and Shavon had no mother or father to protect them in this cruel world. All they had was each other.

In the aftermath of the fire, it was determined that the fire was started as a result of faulty electrical wiring in one of the electrical outlets in Raylene's bedroom. The landlord who owned the house, Roger Dandy, had paid unlicensed electricians to do the electrical work when he bought the house and rehabbed it. As a result of his negligence and refusal to pay a licensed electrician to do the work properly, Jericho's mother was dead and he and his sister were now orphans. They both couldn't understand why their mother had to die and why their father wasn't around to take care of them when they needed him so badly. They were two children who were forced to try to make sense out of a tragedy that not even mature adults could logically explain.

Jericho and Shavon were placed in the care of their maternal grandparents. They moved in with them in their tiny row house in East Baltimore. Their grandparents, Robert and Deborah Jones, received a check from the State to assist them financially with providing for Jericho and Shavon's essential needs. The two siblings never had much of a relationship with their grandparents prior to their mother's death and that didn't change much once they moved into their home. His mother told him that they disowned her when she became involved with their father. They grew up in America in a time period where interracial relationships were taboo. They were ashamed to see their daughter romantically involved with a White man, whom they considered to be the enemy of black people. It was clear to Jericho and Shavon that the only reason that their grandparents took them in was out of social obligation as opposed to love. They were treated like tenants as opposed to their grandchildren. The two of them grew closer with each other, but remained distant from their grandparents.

When his mother died, so too did Jericho's sense of human compassion. He became cold hearted and prone to violence. The littlest things would set him off. He was mad with the world and wondered what he could have possibly done as a child to deserve for his mother to die such a painful death..........